GRAPHIC
NOVEL
CLASSICS

SHERLOCK HOLMES
THE HOUND OF THE BASKERVILLES

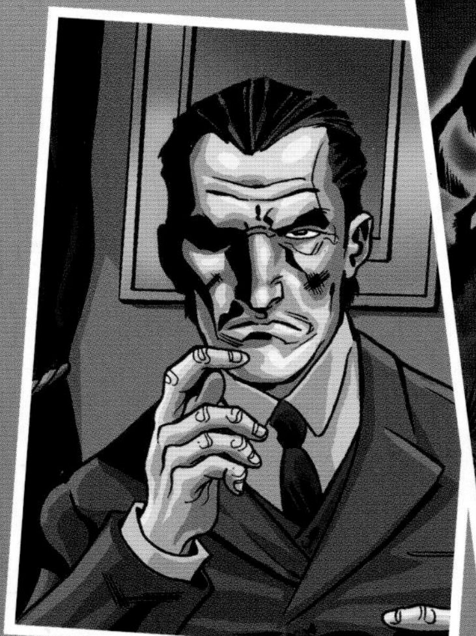
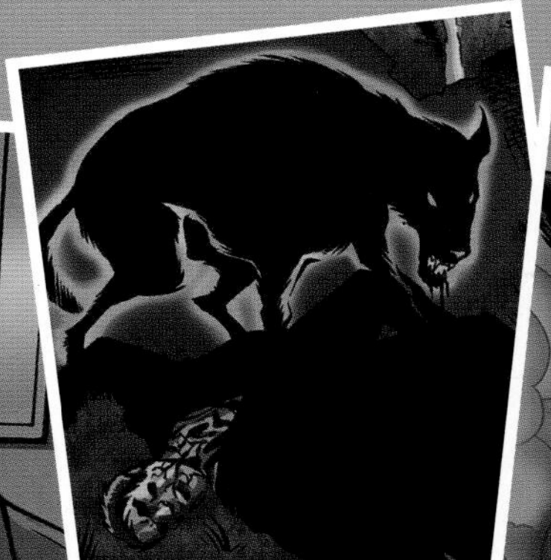
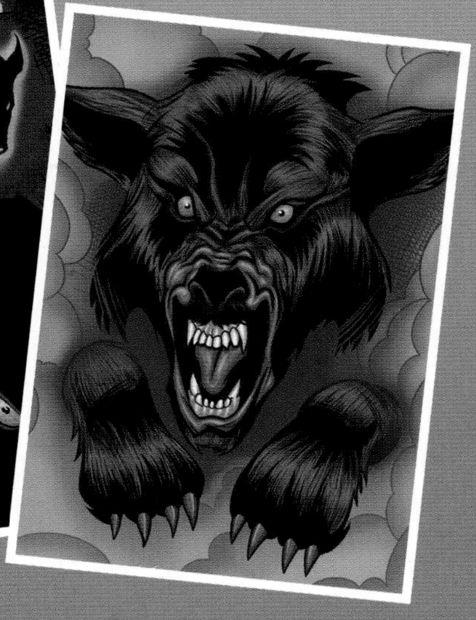

SIR ARTHUR CONAN DOYLE

ARCTURUS

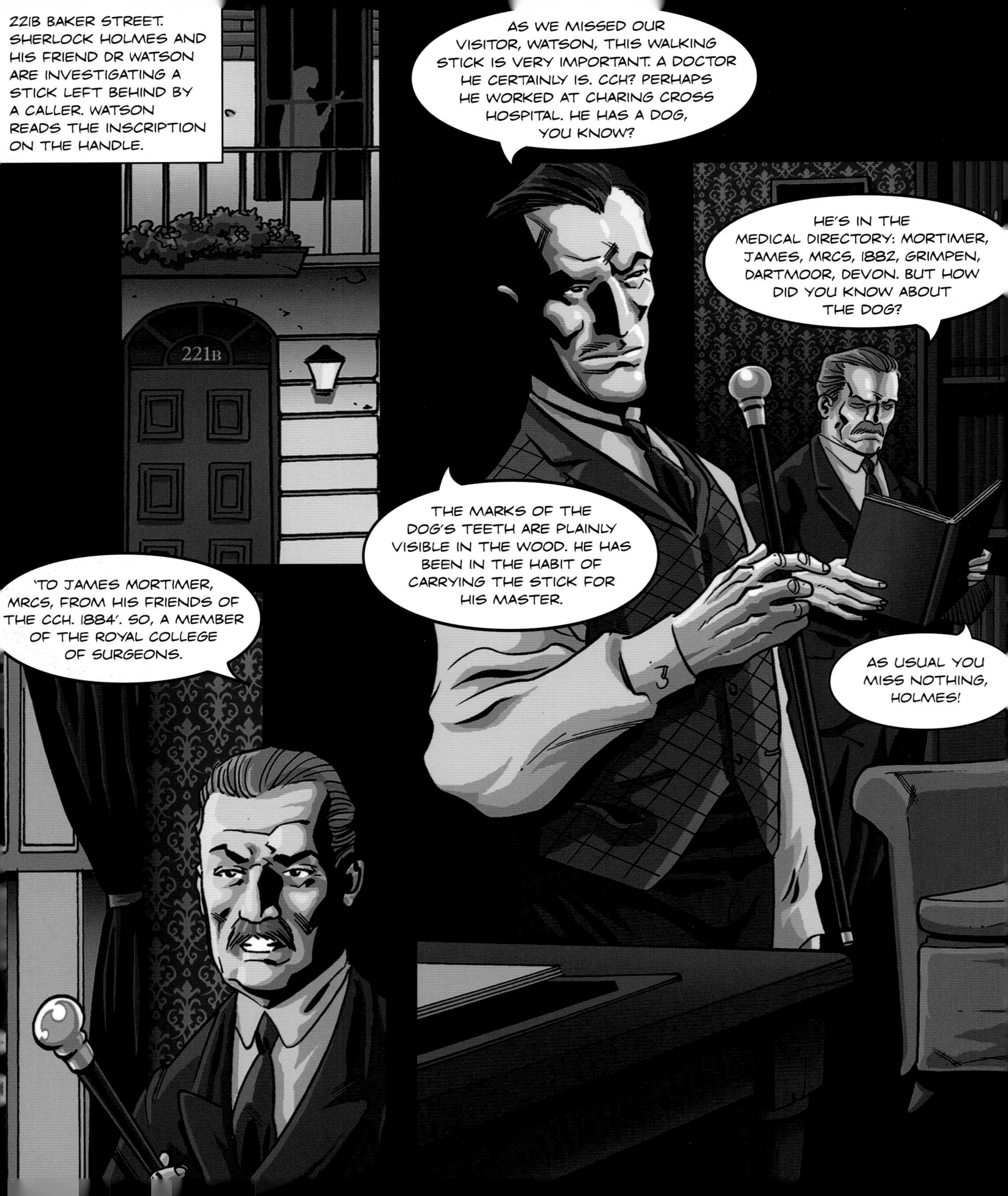
221B BAKER STREET. SHERLOCK HOLMES AND HIS FRIEND DR WATSON ARE INVESTIGATING A STICK LEFT BEHIND BY A CALLER. WATSON READS THE INSCRIPTION ON THE HANDLE.
221B
'TO JAMES MORTIMER, MRCS, FROM HIS FRIENDS OF THE CCH. 1884'. SO, A MEMBER OF THE ROYAL COLLEGE OF SURGEONS.
AS WE MISSED OUR VISITOR, WATSON, THIS WALKING STICK IS VERY IMPORTANT. A DOCTOR HE CERTAINLY IS. CCH? PERHAPS HE WORKED AT CHARING CROSS HOSPITAL. HE HAS A DOG, YOU KNOW?
HE'S IN THE MEDICAL DIRECTORY: MORTIMER, JAMES, MRCS, 1882, GRIMPEN, DARTMOOR, DEVON. BUT HOW DID YOU KNOW ABOUT THE DOG?
THE MARKS OF THE DOG'S TEETH ARE PLAINLY VISIBLE IN THE WOOD. HE HAS BEEN IN THE HABIT OF CARRYING THE STICK FOR HIS MASTER.
AS USUAL YOU MISS NOTHING, HOLMES!

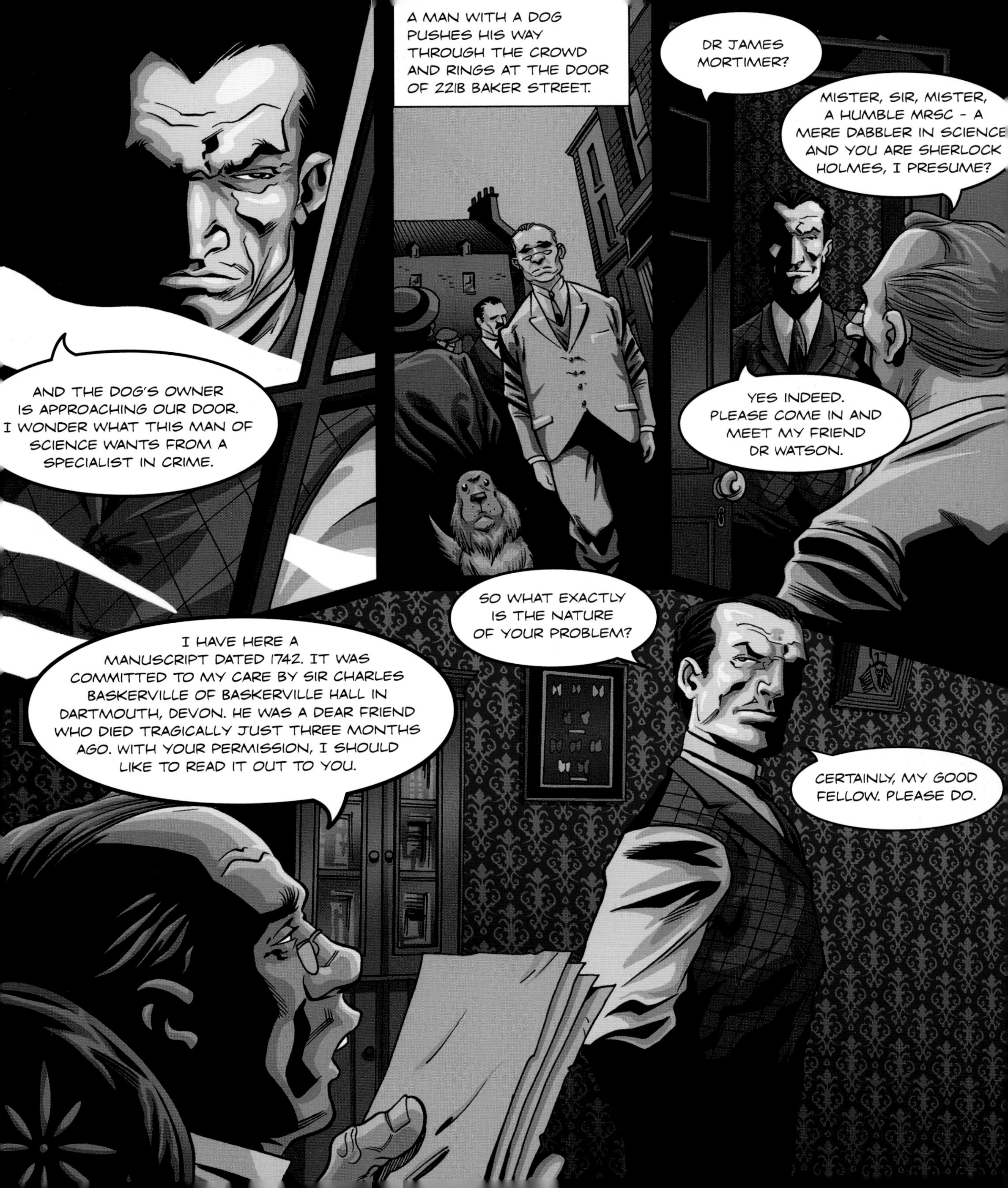
AND THE DOG'S OWNER IS APPROACHING OUR DOOR. I WONDER WHAT THIS MAN OF SCIENCE WANTS FROM A SPECIALIST IN CRIME.
A MAN WITH A DOG PUSHES HIS WAY THROUGH THE CROWD AND RINGS AT THE DOOR OF 221B BAKER STREET.
DR JAMES MORTIMER?
MISTER, SIR, MISTER, A HUMBLE MRSC - A MERE DABBLER IN SCIENCE AND YOU ARE SHERLOCK HOLMES, I PRESUME?
YES INDEED. PLEASE COME IN AND MEET MY FRIEND DR WATSON.
SO WHAT EXACTLY IS THE NATURE OF YOUR PROBLEM?
I HAVE HERE A MANUSCRIPT DATED 1742. IT WAS COMMITTED TO MY CARE BY SIR CHARLES BASKERVILLE OF BASKERVILLE HALL IN DARTMOUTH, DEVON. HE WAS A DEAR FRIEND WHO DIED TRAGICALLY JUST THREE MONTHS AGO. WITH YOUR PERMISSION, I SHOULD LIKE TO READ IT OUT TO YOU.
CERTAINLY, MY GOOD FELLOW. PLEASE DO.

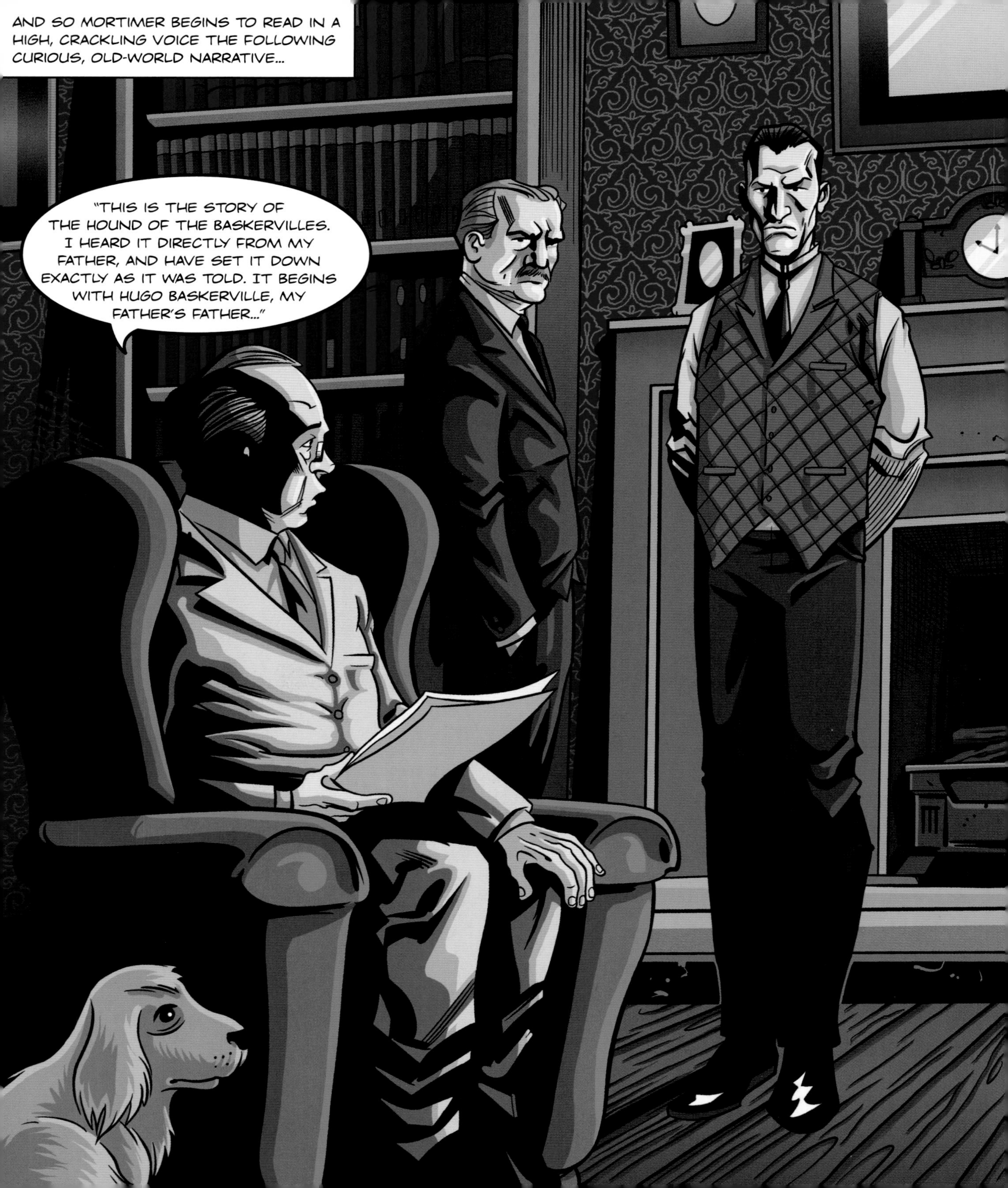
AND SO MORTIMER BEGINS TO READ IN A HIGH, CRACKLING VOICE THE FOLLOWING CURIOUS, OLD-WORLD NARRATIVE...
"THIS IS THE STORY OF THE HOUND OF THE BASKERVILLES. I HEARD IT DIRECTLY FROM MY FATHER, AND HAVE SET IT DOWN EXACTLY AS IT WAS TOLD. IT BEGINS WITH HUGO BASKERVILLE, MY FATHER'S FATHER..."

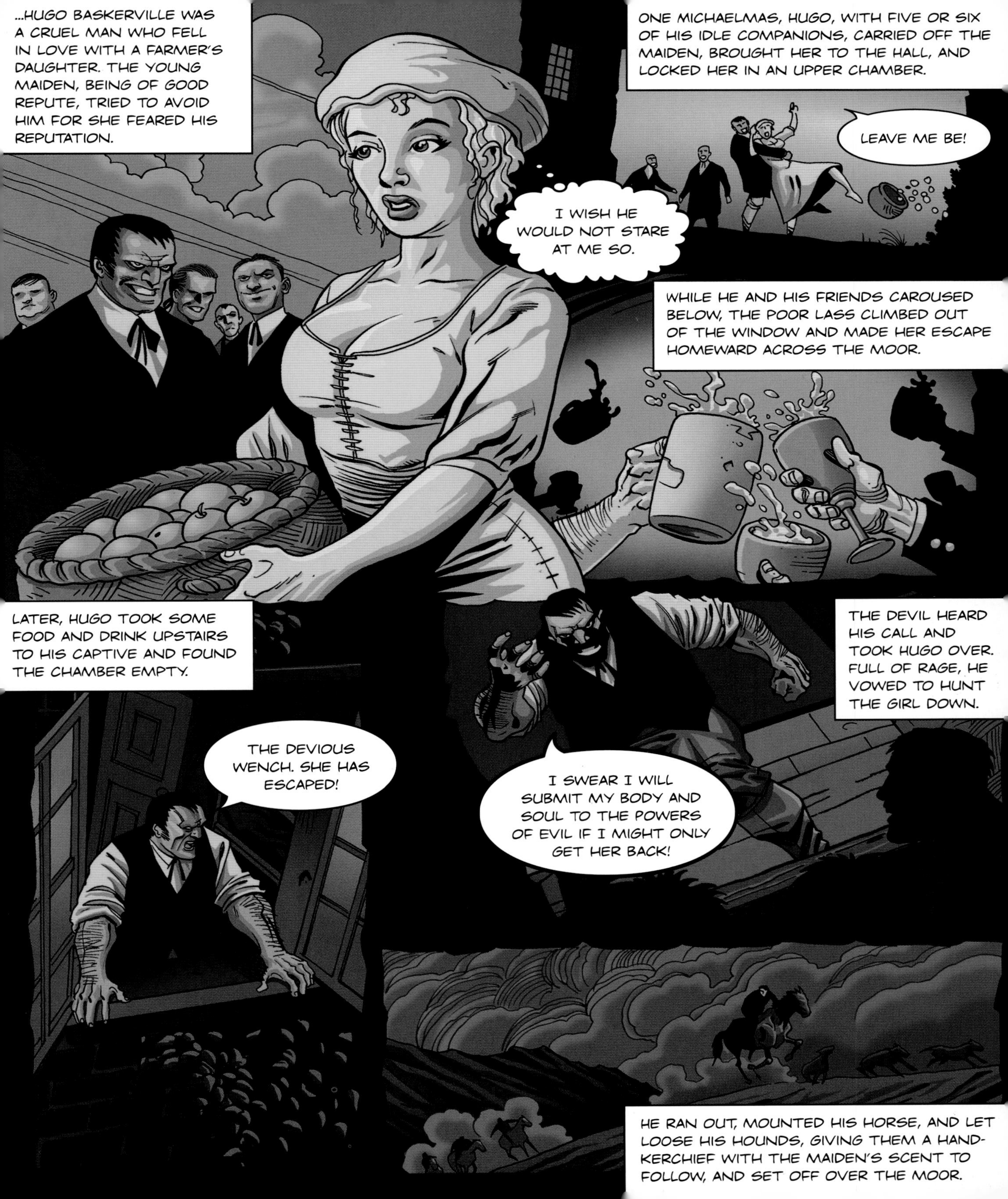
...HUGO BASKERVILLE WAS A CRUEL MAN WHO FELL IN LOVE WITH A FARMER'S DAUGHTER. THE YOUNG MAIDEN, BEING OF GOOD REPUTE, TRIED TO AVOID HIM FOR SHE FEARED HIS REPUTATION.
I WISH HE WOULD NOT STARE AT ME SO.
ONE MICHAELMAS, HUGO, WITH FIVE OR SIX OF HIS IDLE COMPANIONS, CARRIED OFF THE MAIDEN, BROUGHT HER TO THE HALL, AND LOCKED HER IN AN UPPER CHAMBER.
LEAVE ME BE!
WHILE HE AND HIS FRIENDS CAROUSED BELOW, THE POOR LASS CLIMBED OUT OF THE WINDOW AND MADE HER ESCAPE HOMEWARD ACROSS THE MOOR.
LATER, HUGO TOOK SOME FOOD AND DRINK UPSTAIRS TO HIS CAPTIVE AND FOUND THE CHAMBER EMPTY.
THE DEVIOUS WENCH. SHE HAS ESCAPED!
I SWEAR I WILL SUBMIT MY BODY AND SOUL TO THE POWERS OF EVIL IF I MIGHT ONLY GET HER BACK!
THE DEVIL HEARD HIS CALL AND TOOK HUGO OVER. FULL OF RAGE, HE VOWED TO HUNT THE GIRL DOWN.
HE RAN OUT, MOUNTED HIS HORSE, AND LET LOOSE HIS HOUNDS, GIVING THEM A HANDKERCHIEF WITH THE MAIDEN'S SCENT TO FOLLOW, AND SET OFF OVER THE MOOR.

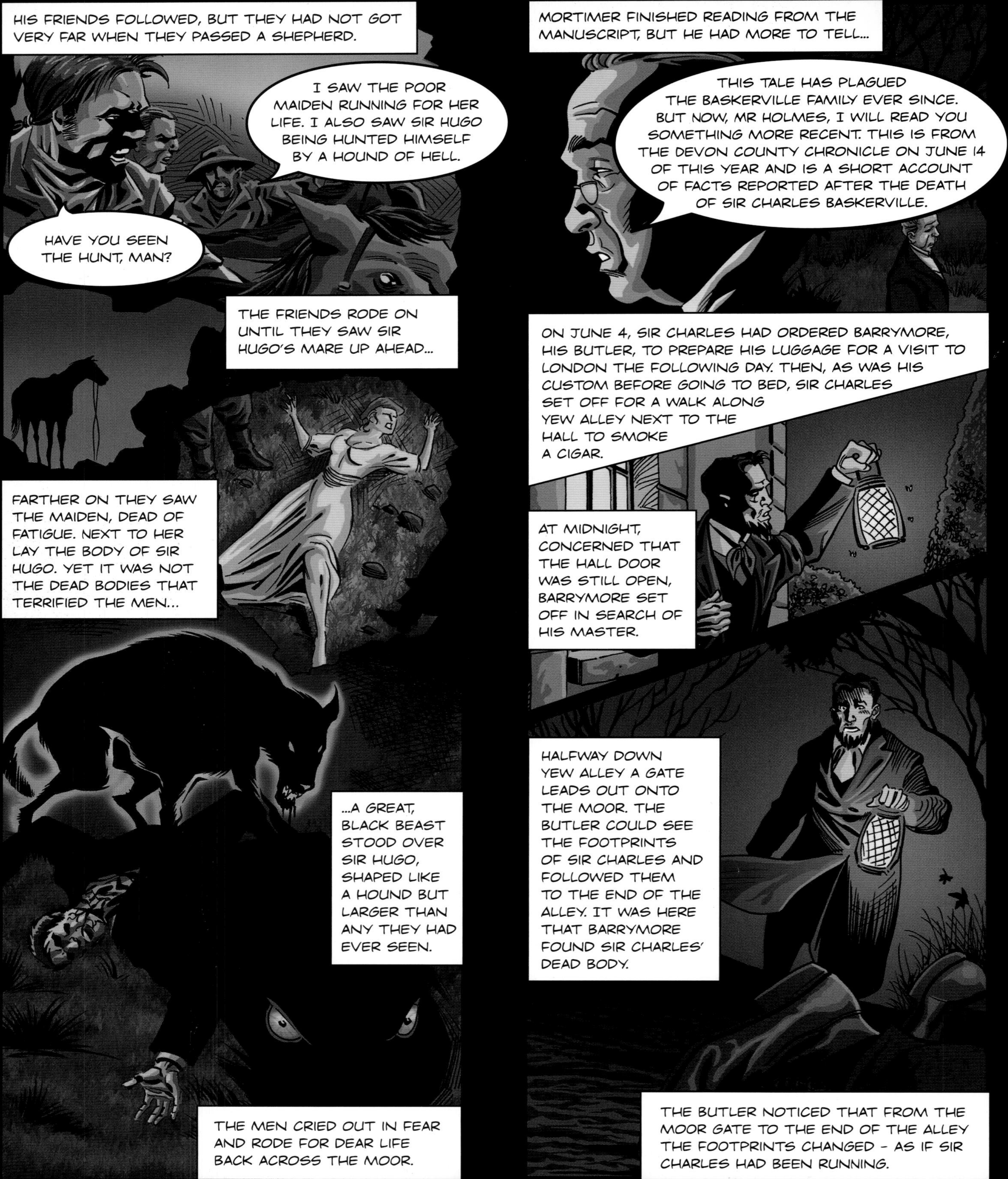
HIS FRIENDS FOLLOWED, BUT THEY HAD NOT GOT VERY FAR WHEN THEY PASSED A SHEPHERD.
HAVE YOU SEEN THE HUNT, MAN?
I SAW THE POOR MAIDEN RUNNING FOR HER LIFE. I ALSO SAW SIR HUGO BEING HUNTED HIMSELF BY A HOUND OF HELL.
THE FRIENDS RODE ON UNTIL THEY SAW SIR HUGO'S MARE UP AHEAD...
FARTHER ON THEY SAW THE MAIDEN, DEAD OF FATIGUE. NEXT TO HER LAY THE BODY OF SIR HUGO. YET IT WAS NOT THE DEAD BODIES THAT TERRIFIED THE MEN...
...A GREAT, BLACK BEAST STOOD OVER SIR HUGO, SHAPED LIKE A HOUND BUT LARGER THAN ANY THEY HAD EVER SEEN.
THE MEN CRIED OUT IN FEAR AND RODE FOR DEAR LIFE BACK ACROSS THE MOOR.
MORTIMER FINISHED READING FROM THE MANUSCRIPT, BUT HE HAD MORE TO TELL...
THIS TALE HAS PLAGUED THE BASKERVILLE FAMILY EVER SINCE. BUT NOW, MR HOLMES, I WILL READ YOU SOMETHING MORE RECENT. THIS IS FROM THE DEVON COUNTY CHRONICLE ON JUNE 14 OF THIS YEAR AND IS A SHORT ACCOUNT OF FACTS REPORTED AFTER THE DEATH OF SIR CHARLES BASKERVILLE.
ON JUNE 4, SIR CHARLES HAD ORDERED BARRYMORE, HIS BUTLER, TO PREPARE HIS LUGGAGE FOR A VISIT TO LONDON THE FOLLOWING DAY. THEN, AS WAS HIS CUSTOM BEFORE GOING TO BED, SIR CHARLES SET OFF FOR A WALK ALONG YEW ALLEY NEXT TO THE HALL TO SMOKE A CIGAR.
AT MIDNIGHT, CONCERNED THAT THE HALL DOOR WAS STILL OPEN, BARRYMORE SET OFF IN SEARCH OF HIS MASTER.
HALFWAY DOWN YEW ALLEY A GATE LEADS OUT ONTO THE MOOR. THE BUTLER COULD SEE THE FOOTPRINTS OF SIR CHARLES AND FOLLOWED THEM TO THE END OF THE ALLEY. IT WAS HERE THAT BARRYMORE FOUND SIR CHARLES' DEAD BODY.
THE BUTLER NOTICED THAT FROM THE MOOR GATE TO THE END OF THE ALLEY THE FOOTPRINTS CHANGED - AS IF SIR CHARLES HAD BEEN RUNNING.

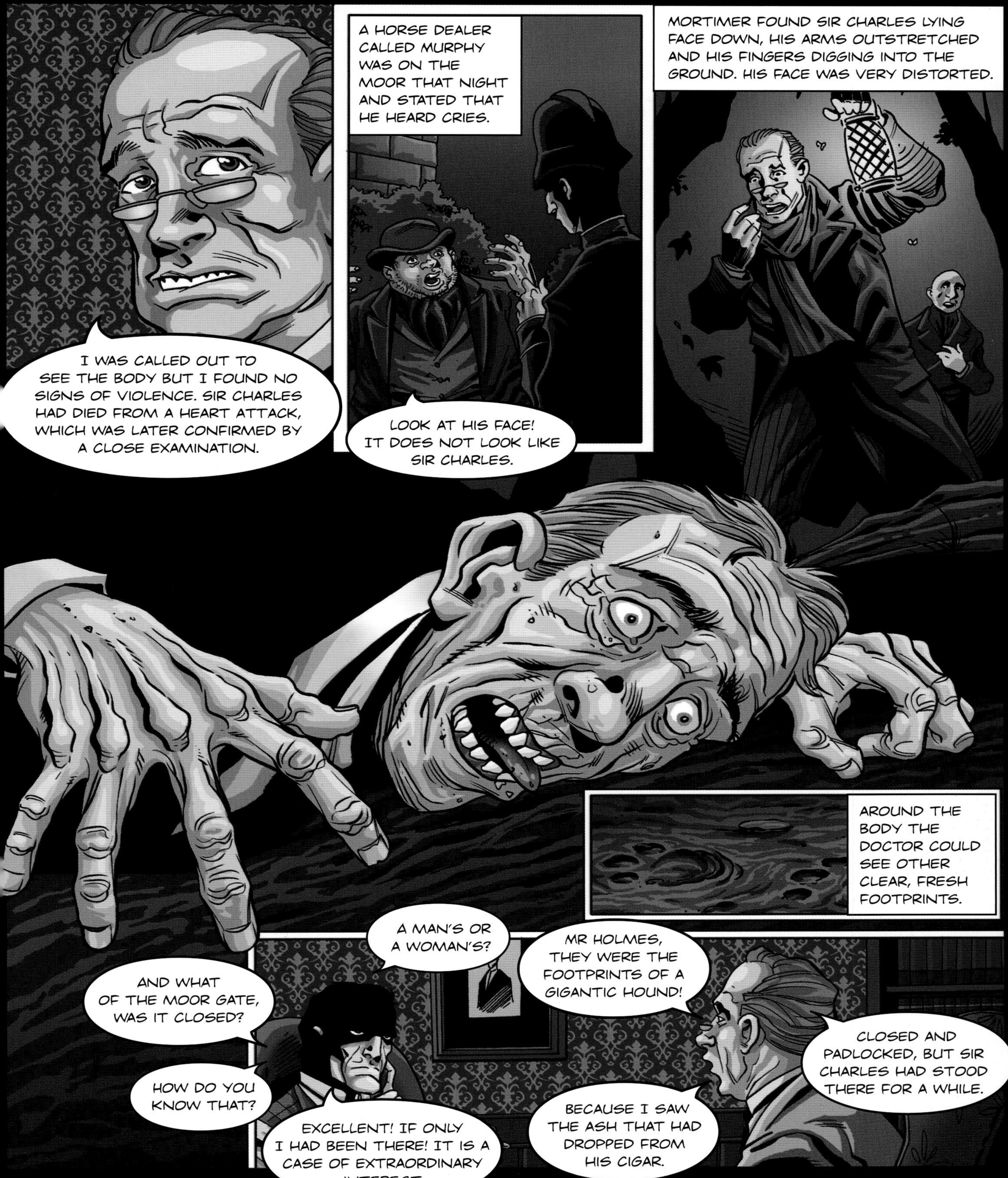
I WAS CALLED OUT TO SEE THE BODY BUT I FOUND NO SIGNS OF VIOLENCE. SIR CHARLES HAD DIED FROM A HEART ATTACK, WHICH WAS LATER CONFIRMED BY A CLOSE EXAMINATION.
A HORSE DEALER CALLED MURPHY WAS ON THE MOOR THAT NIGHT AND STATED THAT HE HEARD CRIES.
LOOK AT HIS FACE! IT DOES NOT LOOK LIKE SIR CHARLES.
MORTIMER FOUND SIR CHARLES LYING FACE DOWN, HIS ARMS OUTSTRETCHED AND HIS FINGERS DIGGING INTO THE GROUND. HIS FACE WAS VERY DISTORTED.
AROUND THE BODY THE DOCTOR COULD SEE OTHER CLEAR, FRESH FOOTPRINTS.
A MAN'S OR A WOMAN'S?
MR HOLMES, THEY WERE THE FOOTPRINTS OF A GIGANTIC HOUND!
AND WHAT OF THE MOOR GATE, WAS IT CLOSED?
CLOSED AND PADLOCKED, BUT SIR CHARLES HAD STOOD THERE FOR A WHILE.
HOW DO YOU KNOW THAT?
BECAUSE I SAW THE ASH THAT HAD DROPPED FROM HIS CIGAR.
EXCELLENT! IF ONLY I HAD BEEN THERE! IT IS A CASE OF EXTRAORDINARY INTEREST.

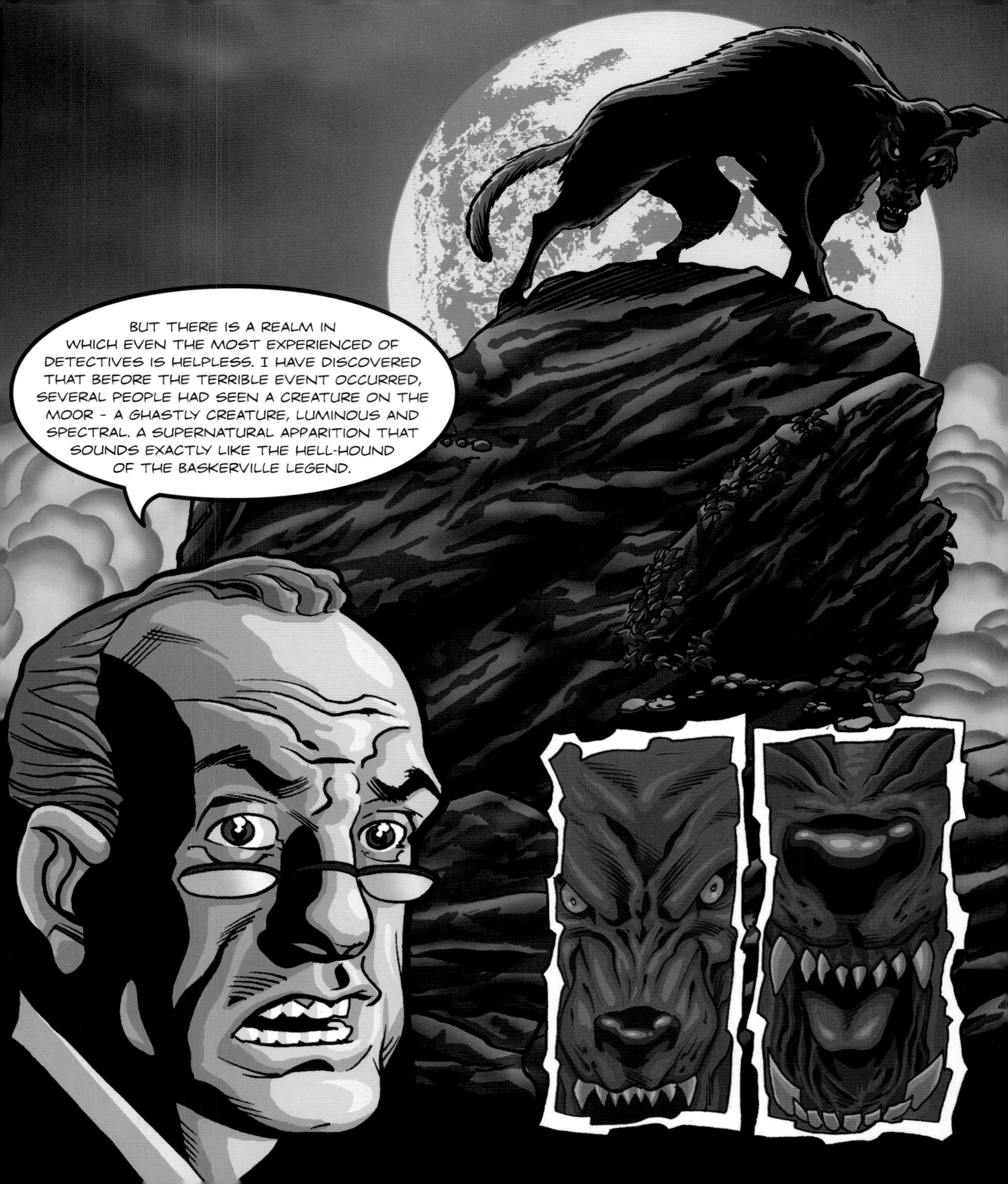
BUT THERE IS A REALM IN WHICH EVEN THE MOST EXPERIENCED OF DETECTIVES IS HELPLESS. I HAVE DISCOVERED THAT BEFORE THE TERRIBLE EVENT OCCURRED, SEVERAL PEOPLE HAD SEEN A CREATURE ON THE MOOR - A GHASTLY CREATURE, LUMINOUS AND SPECTRAL. A SUPERNATURAL APPARITION THAT SOUNDS EXACTLY LIKE THE HELL-HOUND OF THE BASKERVILLE LEGEND.

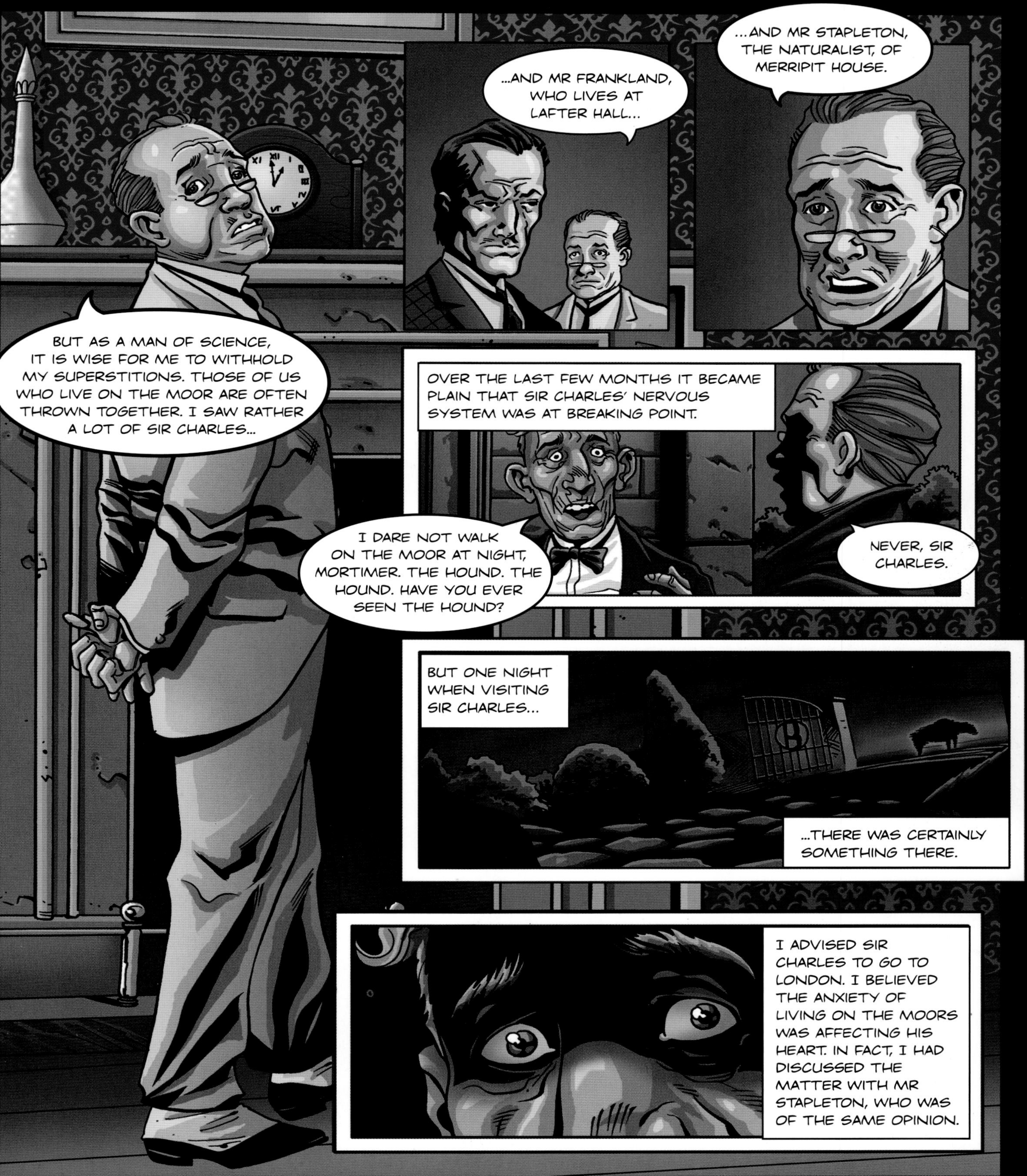
...AND MR FRANKLAND, WHO LIVES AT LAFTER HALL...
...AND MR STAPLETON, THE NATURALIST, OF MERRIPIT HOUSE.
BUT AS A MAN OF SCIENCE, IT IS WISE FOR ME TO WITHHOLD MY SUPERSTITIONS. THOSE OF US WHO LIVE ON THE MOOR ARE OFTEN THROWN TOGETHER. I SAW RATHER A LOT OF SIR CHARLES...
OVER THE LAST FEW MONTHS IT BECAME PLAIN THAT SIR CHARLES' NERVOUS SYSTEM WAS AT BREAKING POINT.
I DARE NOT WALK ON THE MOOR AT NIGHT, MORTIMER. THE HOUND. THE HOUND. HAVE YOU EVER SEEN THE HOUND?
NEVER, SIR CHARLES.
BUT ONE NIGHT WHEN VISITING SIR CHARLES...
...THERE WAS CERTAINLY SOMETHING THERE.
I ADVISED SIR CHARLES TO GO TO LONDON. I BELIEVED THE ANXIETY OF LIVING ON THE MOORS WAS AFFECTING HIS HEART. IN FACT, I HAD DISCUSSED THE MATTER WITH MR STAPLETON, WHO WAS OF THE SAME OPINION.

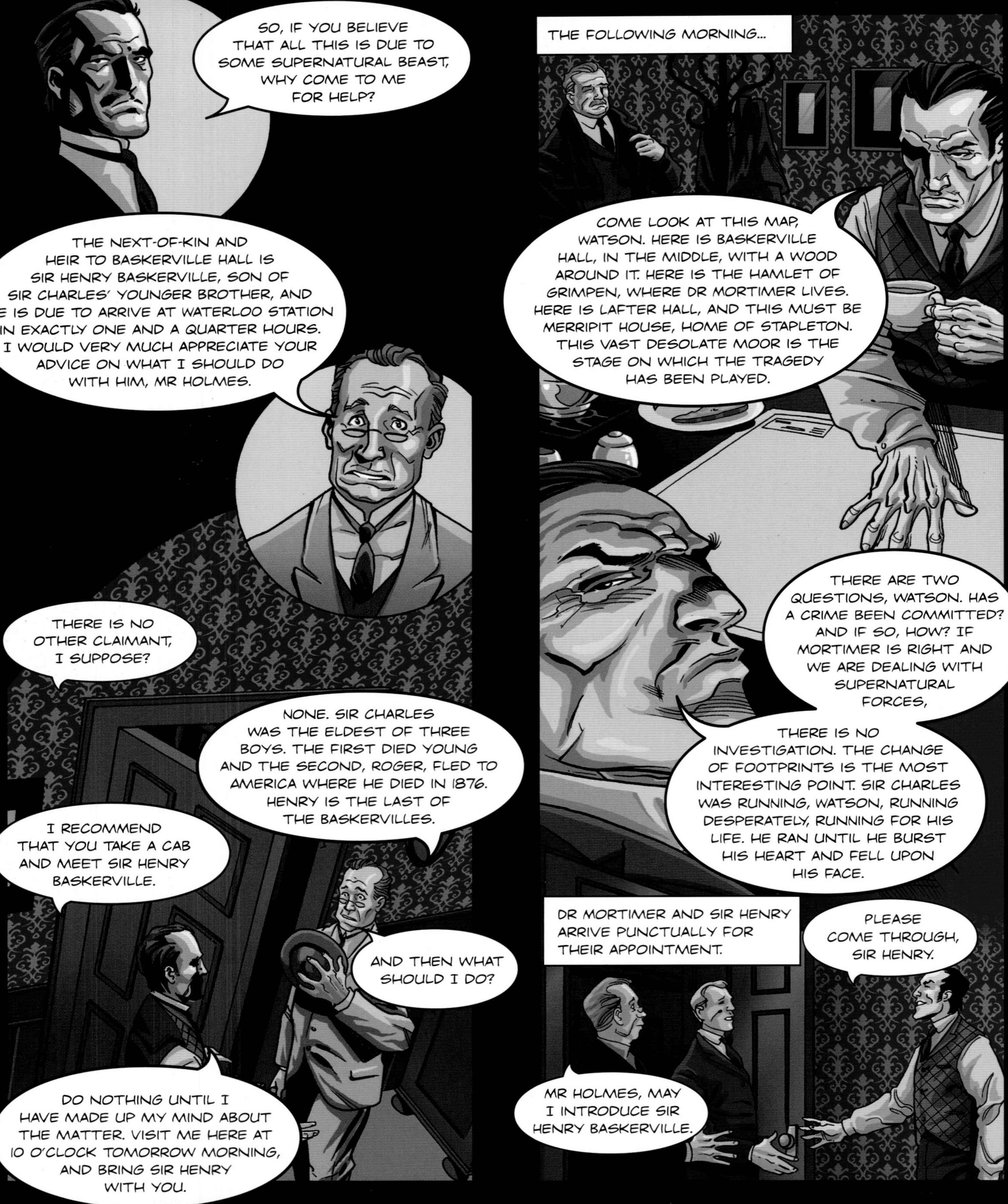
SO, IF YOU BELIEVE THAT ALL THIS IS DUE TO SOME SUPERNATURAL BEAST, WHY COME TO ME FOR HELP?
THE NEXT-OF-KIN AND HEIR TO BASKERVILLE HALL IS SIR HENRY BASKERVILLE, SON OF SIR CHARLES' YOUNGER BROTHER, AND HE IS DUE TO ARRIVE AT WATERLOO STATION IN EXACTLY ONE AND A QUARTER HOURS. I WOULD VERY MUCH APPRECIATE YOUR ADVICE ON WHAT I SHOULD DO WITH HIM, MR HOLMES.
THERE IS NO OTHER CLAIMANT, I SUPPOSE?
NONE. SIR CHARLES WAS THE ELDEST OF THREE BOYS. THE FIRST DIED YOUNG AND THE SECOND, ROGER, FLED TO AMERICA WHERE HE DIED IN 1876. HENRY IS THE LAST OF THE BASKERVILLES.
I RECOMMEND THAT YOU TAKE A CAB AND MEET SIR HENRY BASKERVILLE.
AND THEN WHAT SHOULD I DO?
DO NOTHING UNTIL I HAVE MADE UP MY MIND ABOUT THE MATTER. VISIT ME HERE AT 10 O'CLOCK TOMORROW MORNING, AND BRING SIR HENRY WITH YOU.
THE FOLLOWING MORNING...
COME LOOK AT THIS MAP, WATSON. HERE IS BASKERVILLE HALL, IN THE MIDDLE, WITH A WOOD AROUND IT. HERE IS THE HAMLET OF GRIMPEN, WHERE DR MORTIMER LIVES. HERE IS LAFTER HALL, AND THIS MUST BE MERRIPIT HOUSE, HOME OF STAPLETON. THIS VAST DESOLATE MOOR IS THE STAGE ON WHICH THE TRAGEDY HAS BEEN PLAYED.
THERE ARE TWO QUESTIONS, WATSON. HAS A CRIME BEEN COMMITTED? AND IF SO, HOW? IF MORTIMER IS RIGHT AND WE ARE DEALING WITH SUPERNATURAL FORCES,
THERE IS NO INVESTIGATION. THE CHANGE OF FOOTPRINTS IS THE MOST INTERESTING POINT. SIR CHARLES WAS RUNNING, WATSON, RUNNING DESPERATELY, RUNNING FOR HIS LIFE. HE RAN UNTIL HE BURST HIS HEART AND FELL UPON HIS FACE.
DR MORTIMER AND SIR HENRY ARRIVE PUNCTUALLY FOR THEIR APPOINTMENT.
PLEASE COME THROUGH, SIR HENRY.
MR HOLMES, MAY I INTRODUCE SIR HENRY BASKERVILLE.

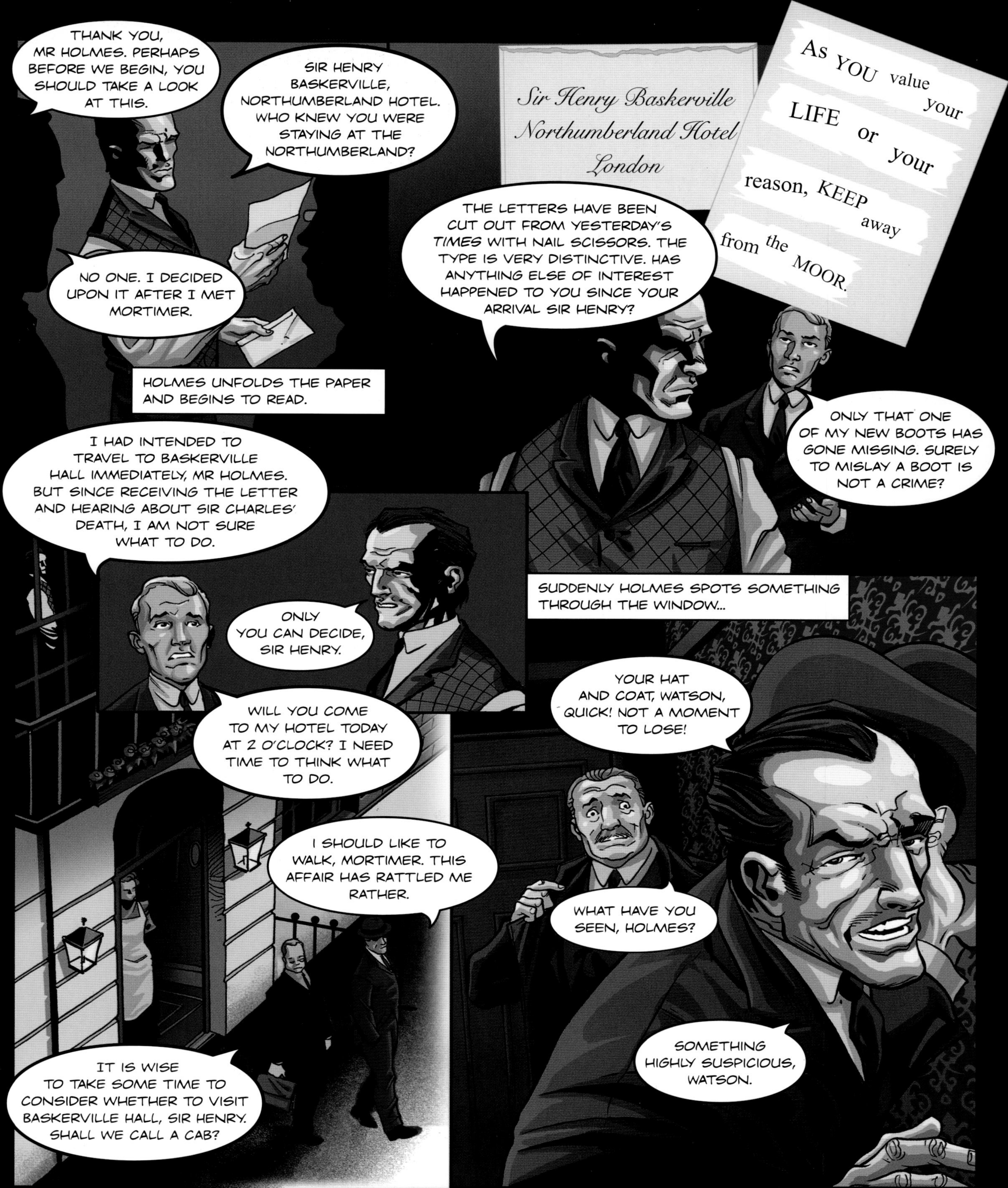
THANK YOU, MR HOLMES. PERHAPS BEFORE WE BEGIN, YOU SHOULD TAKE A LOOK AT THIS.
SIR HENRY BASKERVILLE, NORTHUMBERLAND HOTEL. WHO KNEW YOU WERE STAYING AT THE NORTHUMBERLAND?
NO ONE. I DECIDED UPON IT AFTER I MET MORTIMER.
HOLMES UNFOLDS THE PAPER AND BEGINS TO READ.
Sir Henry Baskerville
Northumberland Hotel
London
As YOU value your LIFE or your reason, KEEP away from the MOOR.
THE LETTERS HAVE BEEN CUT OUT FROM YESTERDAY'S TIMES WITH NAIL SCISSORS. THE TYPE IS VERY DISTINCTIVE. HAS ANYTHING ELSE OF INTEREST HAPPENED TO YOU SINCE YOUR ARRIVAL SIR HENRY?
ONLY THAT ONE OF MY NEW BOOTS HAS GONE MISSING. SURELY TO MISLAY A BOOT IS NOT A CRIME?
I HAD INTENDED TO TRAVEL TO BASKERVILLE HALL IMMEDIATELY, MR HOLMES. BUT SINCE RECEIVING THE LETTER AND HEARING ABOUT SIR CHARLES' DEATH, I AM NOT SURE WHAT TO DO.
ONLY YOU CAN DECIDE, SIR HENRY.
WILL YOU COME TO MY HOTEL TODAY AT 2 O'CLOCK? I NEED TIME TO THINK WHAT TO DO.
I SHOULD LIKE TO WALK, MORTIMER. THIS AFFAIR HAS RATTLED ME RATHER.
IT IS WISE TO TAKE SOME TIME TO CONSIDER WHETHER TO VISIT BASKERVILLE HALL, SIR HENRY. SHALL WE CALL A CAB?
SUDDENLY HOLMES SPOTS SOMETHING THROUGH THE WINDOW...
YOUR HAT AND COAT, WATSON, QUICK! NOT A MOMENT TO LOSE!
WHAT HAVE YOU SEEN, HOLMES?
SOMETHING HIGHLY SUSPICIOUS, WATSON.

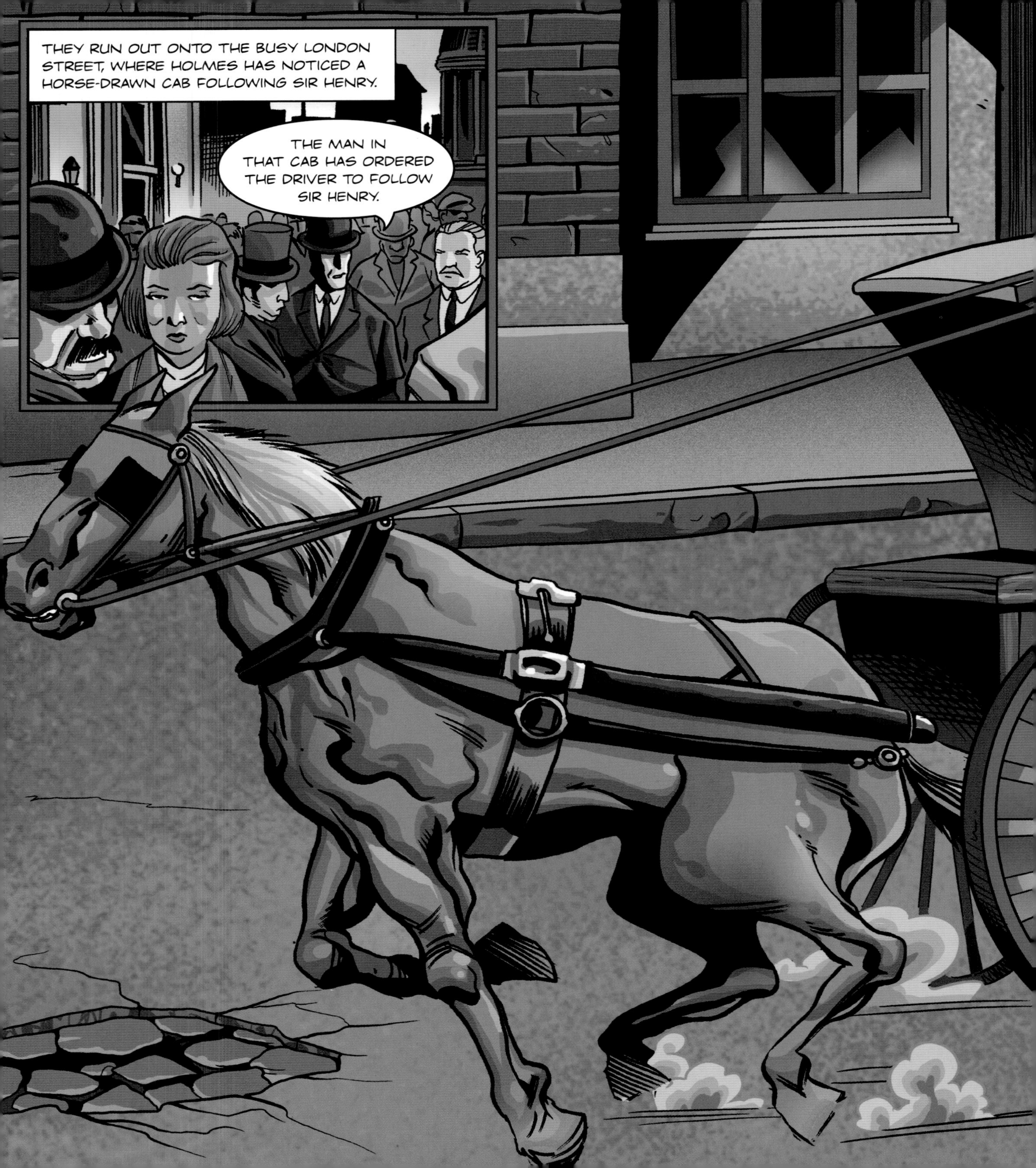
THEY RUN OUT ONTO THE BUSY LONDON STREET, WHERE HOLMES HAS NOTICED A HORSE-DRAWN CAB FOLLOWING SIR HENRY.
THE MAN IN THAT CAB HAS ORDERED THE DRIVER TO FOLLOW SIR HENRY.

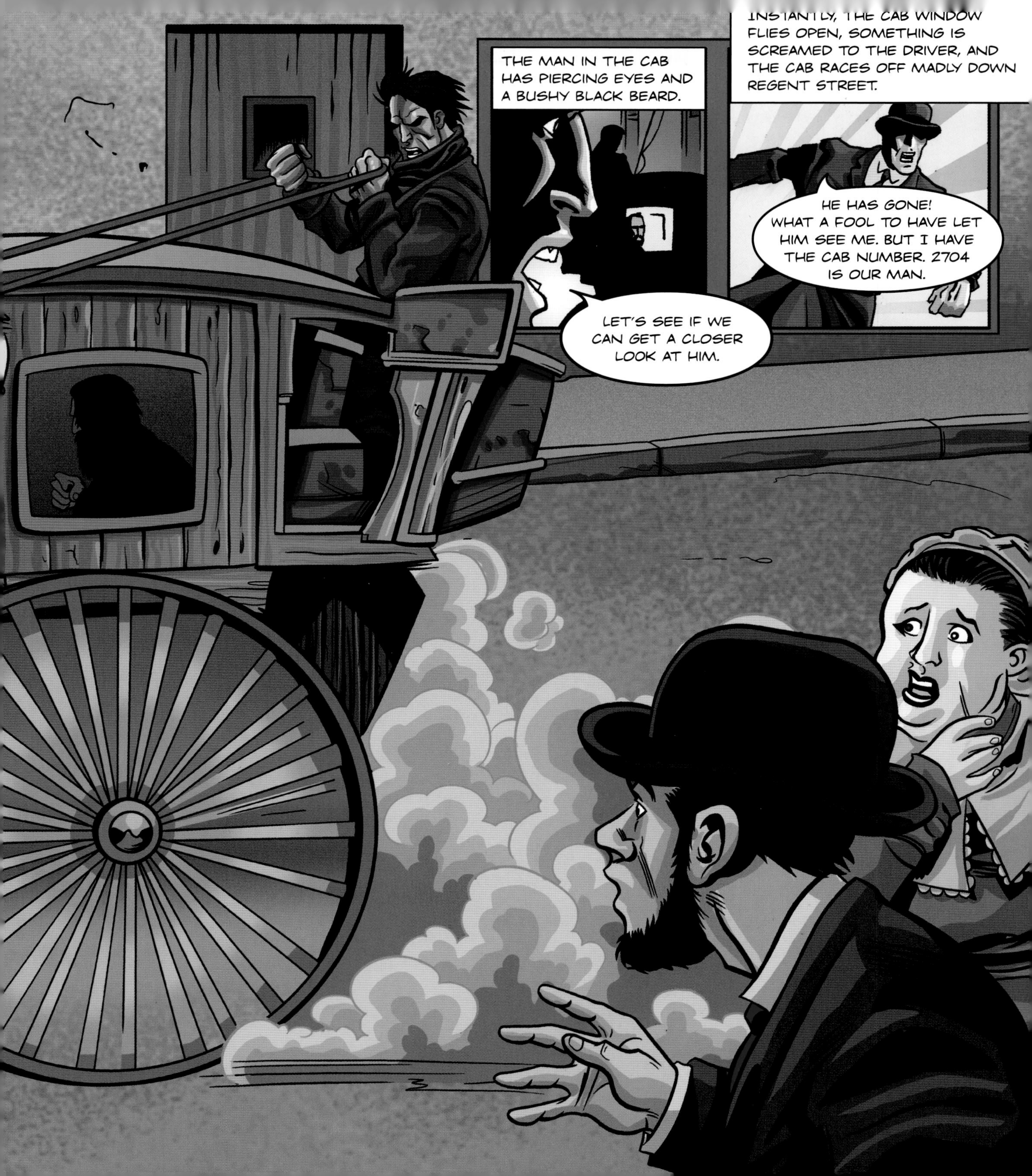
THE MAN IN THE CAB HAS PIERCING EYES AND A BUSHY BLACK BEARD.
LET'S SEE IF WE CAN GET A CLOSER LOOK AT HIM.
INSTANTLY, THE CAB WINDOW FLIES OPEN, SOMETHING IS SCREAMED TO THE DRIVER, AND THE CAB RACES OFF MADLY DOWN REGENT STREET.
HE HAS GONE! WHAT A FOOL TO HAVE LET HIM SEE ME. BUT I HAVE THE CAB NUMBER. 2704 IS OUR MAN.

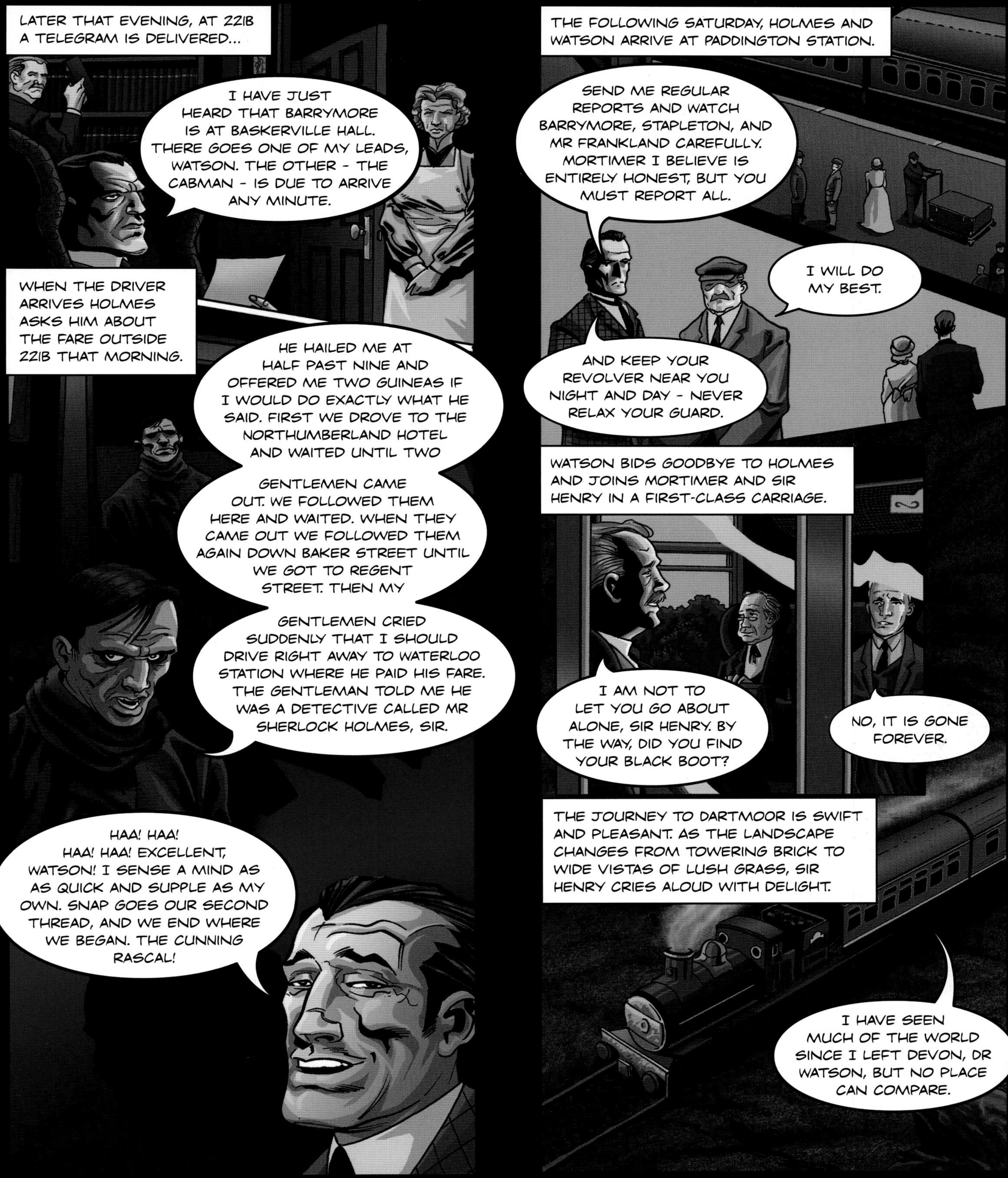
LATER THAT EVENING, AT 221B A TELEGRAM IS DELIVERED...
I HAVE JUST HEARD THAT BARRYMORE IS AT BASKERVILLE HALL. THERE GOES ONE OF MY LEADS, WATSON. THE OTHER - THE CABMAN - IS DUE TO ARRIVE ANY MINUTE.
WHEN THE DRIVER ARRIVES HOLMES ASKS HIM ABOUT THE FARE OUTSIDE 221B THAT MORNING.
HE HAILED ME AT HALF PAST NINE AND OFFERED ME TWO GUINEAS IF I WOULD DO EXACTLY WHAT HE SAID. FIRST WE DROVE TO THE NORTHUMBERLAND HOTEL AND WAITED UNTIL TWO
GENTLEMEN CAME OUT. WE FOLLOWED THEM HERE AND WAITED. WHEN THEY CAME OUT WE FOLLOWED THEM AGAIN DOWN BAKER STREET UNTIL WE GOT TO REGENT STREET. THEN MY
GENTLEMEN CRIED SUDDENLY THAT I SHOULD DRIVE RIGHT AWAY TO WATERLOO STATION WHERE HE PAID HIS FARE. THE GENTLEMAN TOLD ME HE WAS A DETECTIVE CALLED MR SHERLOCK HOLMES, SIR.
HAA! HAA! HAA! HAA! EXCELLENT, WATSON! I SENSE A MIND AS AS QUICK AND SUPPLE AS MY OWN. SNAP GOES OUR SECOND THREAD, AND WE END WHERE WE BEGAN. THE CUNNING RASCAL!
THE FOLLOWING SATURDAY, HOLMES AND WATSON ARRIVE AT PADDINGTON STATION.
SEND ME REGULAR REPORTS AND WATCH BARRYMORE, STAPLETON, AND MR FRANKLAND CAREFULLY. MORTIMER I BELIEVE IS ENTIRELY HONEST, BUT YOU MUST REPORT ALL.
I WILL DO MY BEST.
AND KEEP YOUR REVOLVER NEAR YOU NIGHT AND DAY - NEVER RELAX YOUR GUARD.
WATSON BIDS GOODBYE TO HOLMES AND JOINS MORTIMER AND SIR HENRY IN A FIRST-CLASS CARRIAGE.
I AM NOT TO LET YOU GO ABOUT ALONE, SIR HENRY. BY THE WAY, DID YOU FIND YOUR BLACK BOOT?
NO, IT IS GONE FOREVER.
THE JOURNEY TO DARTMOOR IS SWIFT AND PLEASANT. AS THE LANDSCAPE CHANGES FROM TOWERING BRICK TO WIDE VISTAS OF LUSH GRASS, SIR HENRY CRIES ALOUD WITH DELIGHT.
I HAVE SEEN MUCH OF THE WORLD SINCE I LEFT DEVON, DR WATSON, BUT NO PLACE CAN COMPARE.

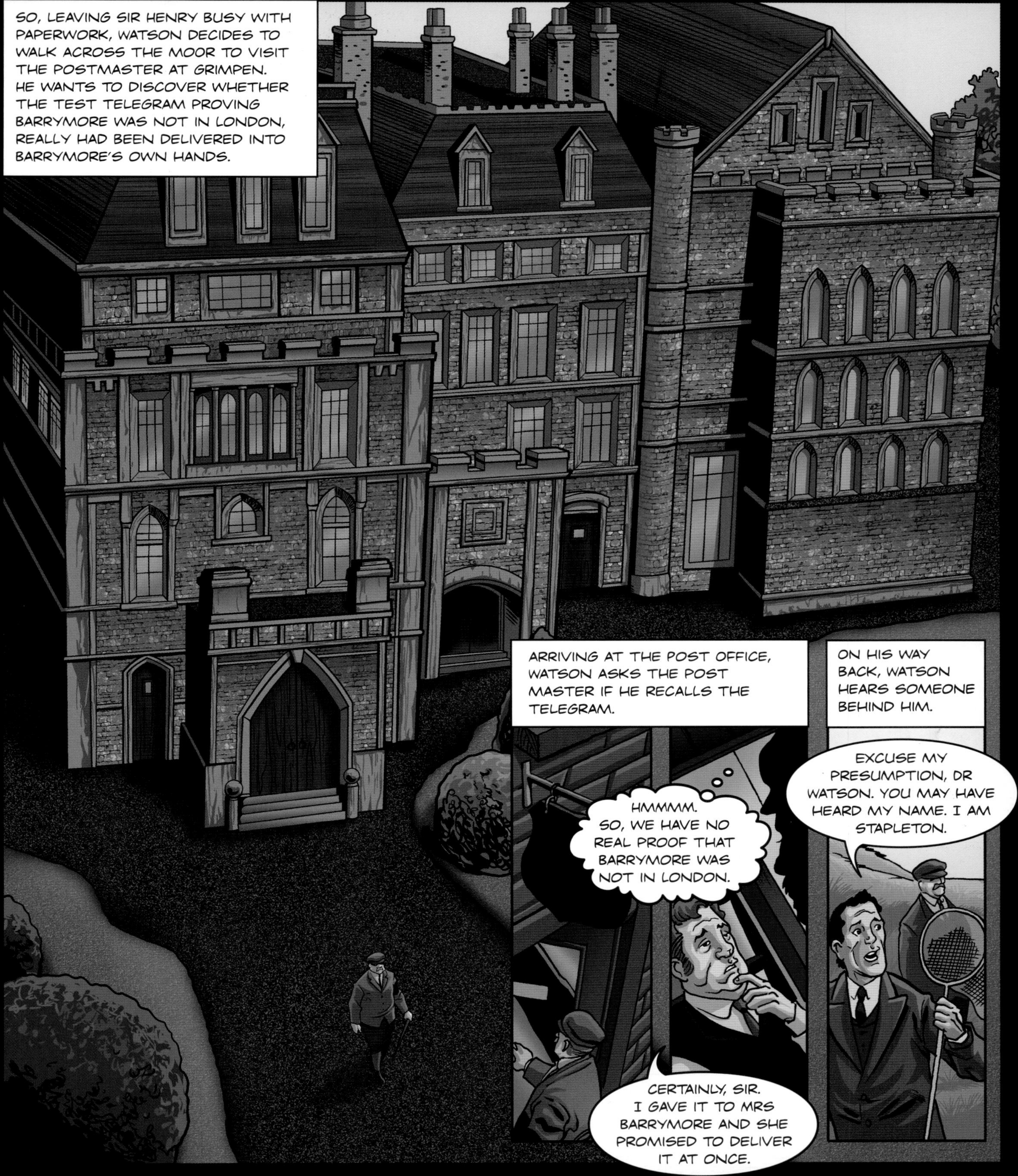
SO, LEAVING SIR HENRY BUSY WITH PAPERWORK, WATSON DECIDES TO WALK ACROSS THE MOOR TO VISIT THE POSTMASTER AT GRIMPEN. HE WANTS TO DISCOVER WHETHER THE TEST TELEGRAM PROVING BARRYMORE WAS NOT IN LONDON, REALLY HAD BEEN DELIVERED INTO BARRYMORE'S OWN HANDS.
ARRIVING AT THE POST OFFICE, WATSON ASKS THE POST MASTER IF HE RECALLS THE TELEGRAM.
CERTAINLY, SIR. I GAVE IT TO MRS BARRYMORE AND SHE PROMISED TO DELIVER IT AT ONCE.
HMMMM. SO, WE HAVE NO REAL PROOF THAT BARRYMORE WAS NOT IN LONDON.
ON HIS WAY BACK, WATSON HEARS SOMEONE BEHIND HIM.
EXCUSE MY PRESUMPTION, DR WATSON. YOU MAY HAVE HEARD MY NAME. I AM STAPLETON.

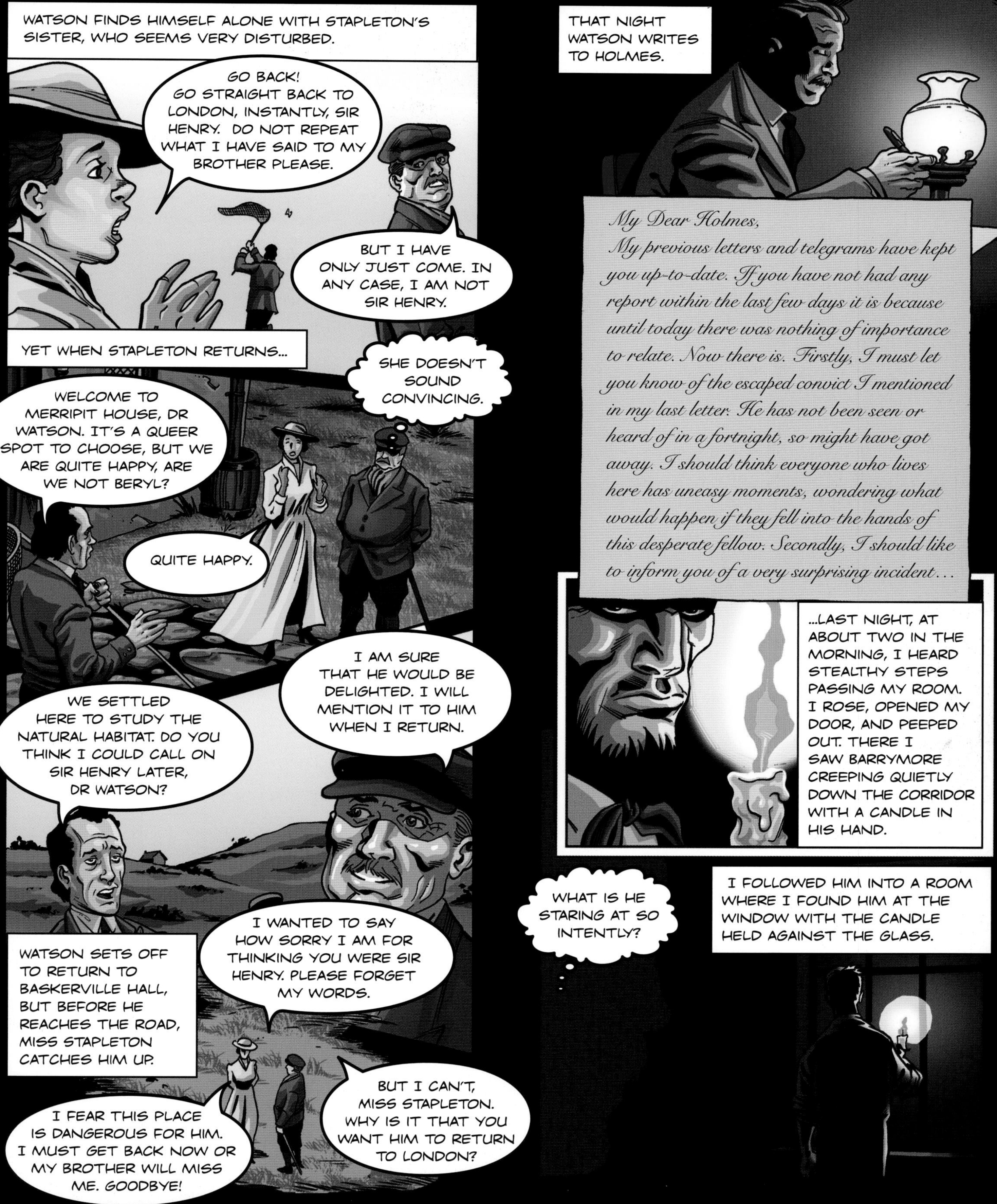
WATSON FINDS HIMSELF ALONE WITH STAPLETON'S SISTER, WHO SEEMS VERY DISTURBED.
GO BACK! GO STRAIGHT BACK TO LONDON, INSTANTLY, SIR HENRY. DO NOT REPEAT WHAT I HAVE SAID TO MY BROTHER PLEASE.
BUT I HAVE ONLY JUST COME. IN ANY CASE, I AM NOT SIR HENRY.
YET WHEN STAPLETON RETURNS...
SHE DOESN'T SOUND CONVINCING.
WELCOME TO MERRIPIT HOUSE, DR WATSON. IT'S A QUEER SPOT TO CHOOSE, BUT WE ARE QUITE HAPPY, ARE WE NOT BERYL?
QUITE HAPPY.
I AM SURE THAT HE WOULD BE DELIGHTED. I WILL MENTION IT TO HIM WHEN I RETURN.
WE SETTLED HERE TO STUDY THE NATURAL HABITAT. DO YOU THINK I COULD CALL ON SIR HENRY LATER, DR WATSON?
WATSON SETS OFF TO RETURN TO BASKERVILLE HALL, BUT BEFORE HE REACHES THE ROAD, MISS STAPLETON CATCHES HIM UP.
I WANTED TO SAY HOW SORRY I AM FOR THINKING YOU WERE SIR HENRY. PLEASE FORGET MY WORDS.
BUT I CAN'T, MISS STAPLETON. WHY IS IT THAT YOU WANT HIM TO RETURN TO LONDON?
I FEAR THIS PLACE IS DANGEROUS FOR HIM. I MUST GET BACK NOW OR MY BROTHER WILL MISS ME. GOODBYE!
THAT NIGHT WATSON WRITES TO HOLMES.
My Dear Holmes,
My previous letters and telegrams have kept you up-to-date. If you have not had any report within the last few days it is because until today there was nothing of importance to relate. Now there is. Firstly, I must let you know of the escaped convict I mentioned in my last letter. He has not been seen or heard of in a fortnight, so might have got away. I should think everyone who lives here has uneasy moments, wondering what would happen if they fell into the hands of this desperate fellow. Secondly, I should like to inform you of a very surprising incident...
...LAST NIGHT, AT ABOUT TWO IN THE MORNING, I HEARD STEALTHY STEPS PASSING MY ROOM. I ROSE, OPENED MY DOOR, AND PEEPED OUT. THERE I SAW BARRYMORE CREEPING QUIETLY DOWN THE CORRIDOR WITH A CANDLE IN HIS HAND.
WHAT IS HE STARING AT SO INTENTLY?
I FOLLOWED HIM INTO A ROOM WHERE I FOUND HIM AT THE WINDOW WITH THE CANDLE HELD AGAINST THE GLASS.

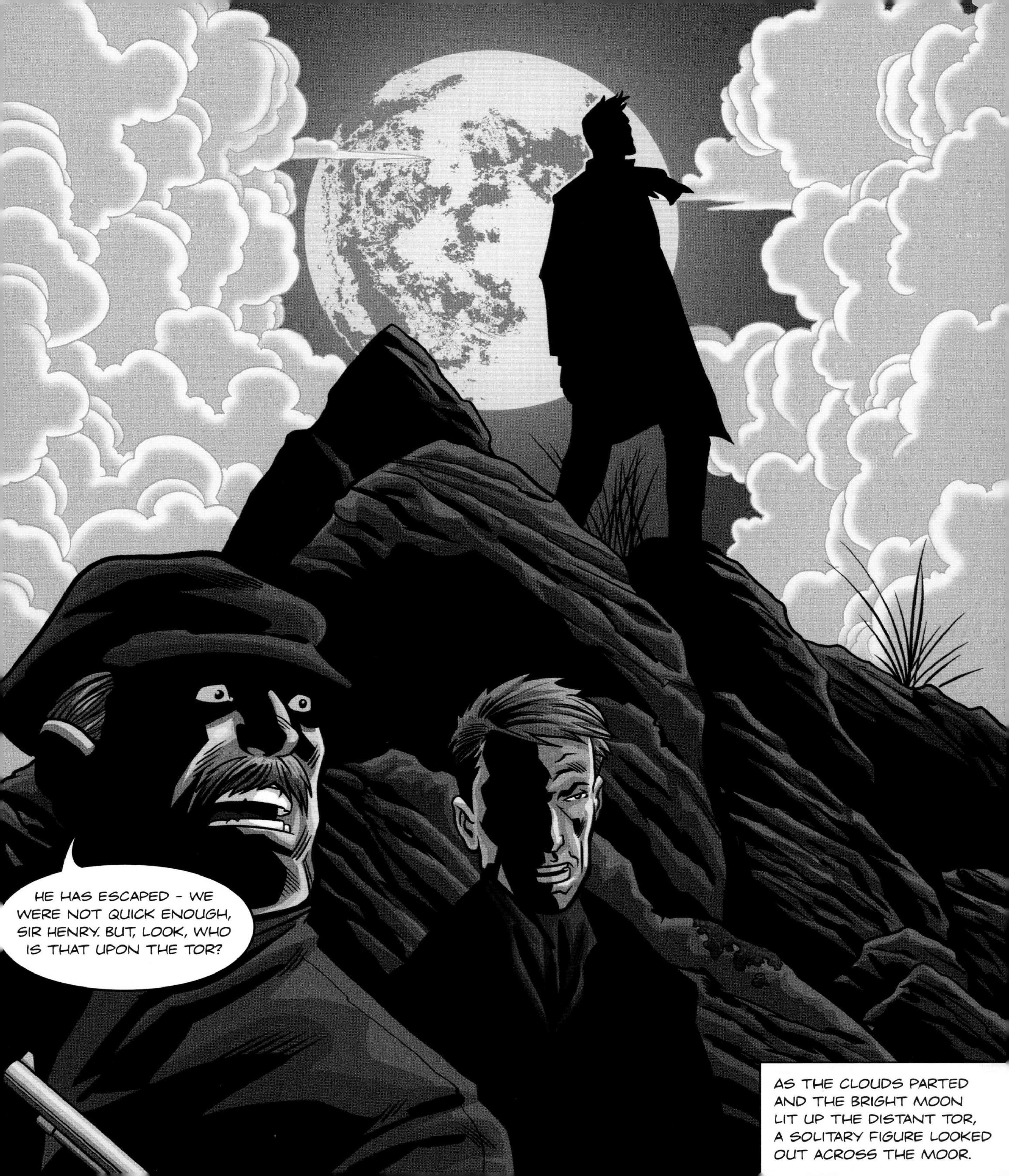
HE HAS ESCAPED - WE WERE NOT QUICK ENOUGH, SIR HENRY. BUT, LOOK, WHO IS THAT UPON THE TOR?
AS THE CLOUDS PARTED AND THE BRIGHT MOON LIT UP THE DISTANT TOR, A SOLITARY FIGURE LOOKED OUT ACROSS THE MOOR.

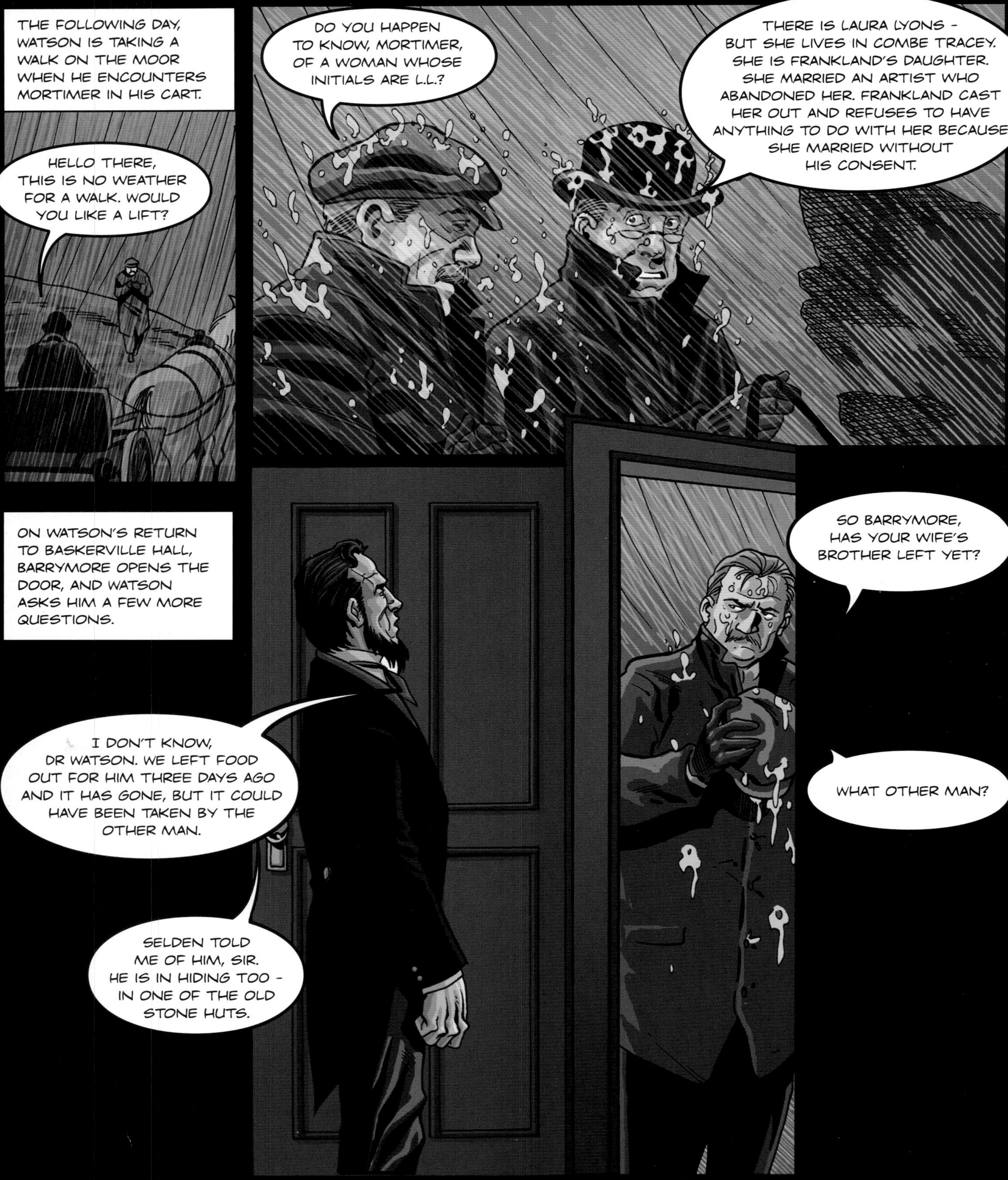
THE FOLLOWING DAY, WATSON IS TAKING A WALK ON THE MOOR WHEN HE ENCOUNTERS MORTIMER IN HIS CART.
HELLO THERE, THIS IS NO WEATHER FOR A WALK. WOULD YOU LIKE A LIFT?
DO YOU HAPPEN TO KNOW, MORTIMER, OF A WOMAN WHOSE INITIALS ARE L.L.?
THERE IS LAURA LYONS - BUT SHE LIVES IN COMBE TRACEY. SHE IS FRANKLAND'S DAUGHTER. SHE MARRIED AN ARTIST WHO ABANDONED HER. FRANKLAND CAST HER OUT AND REFUSES TO HAVE ANYTHING TO DO WITH HER BECAUSE SHE MARRIED WITHOUT HIS CONSENT.
ON WATSON'S RETURN TO BASKERVILLE HALL, BARRYMORE OPENS THE DOOR, AND WATSON ASKS HIM A FEW MORE QUESTIONS.
SO BARRYMORE, HAS YOUR WIFE'S BROTHER LEFT YET?
I DON'T KNOW, DR WATSON. WE LEFT FOOD OUT FOR HIM THREE DAYS AGO AND IT HAS GONE, BUT IT COULD HAVE BEEN TAKEN BY THE OTHER MAN.
WHAT OTHER MAN?
SELDEN TOLD ME OF HIM, SIR. HE IS IN HIDING TOO - IN ONE OF THE OLD STONE HUTS.

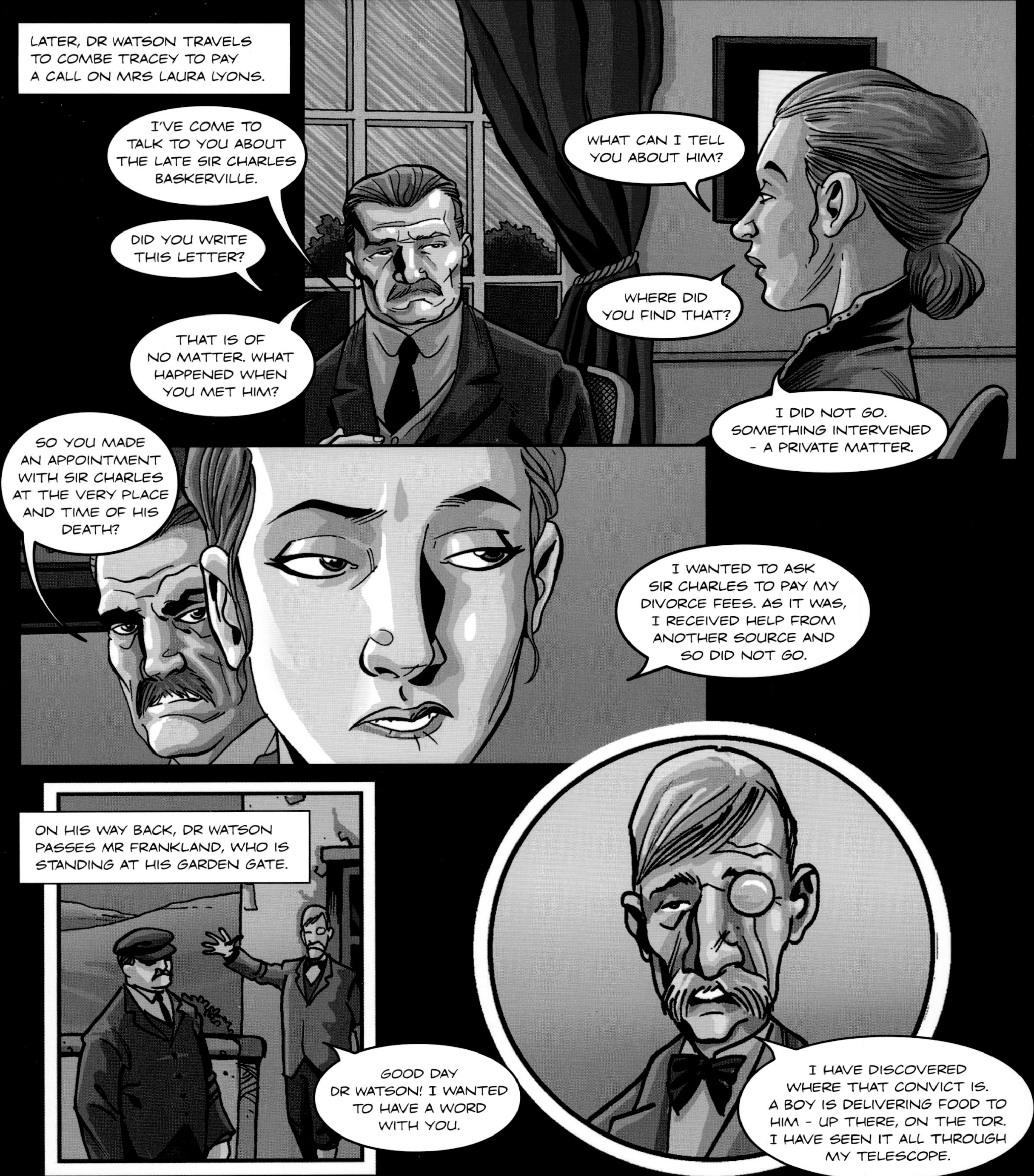
LATER, DR WATSON TRAVELS TO COMBE TRACEY TO PAY A CALL ON MRS LAURA LYONS.
I'VE COME TO TALK TO YOU ABOUT THE LATE SIR CHARLES BASKERVILLE.
WHAT CAN I TELL YOU ABOUT HIM?
DID YOU WRITE THIS LETTER?
WHERE DID YOU FIND THAT?
THAT IS OF NO MATTER. WHAT HAPPENED WHEN YOU MET HIM?
I DID NOT GO. SOMETHING INTERVENED - A PRIVATE MATTER.
SO YOU MADE AN APPOINTMENT WITH SIR CHARLES AT THE VERY PLACE AND TIME OF HIS DEATH?
I WANTED TO ASK SIR CHARLES TO PAY MY DIVORCE FEES. AS IT WAS, I RECEIVED HELP FROM ANOTHER SOURCE AND SO DID NOT GO.
ON HIS WAY BACK, DR WATSON PASSES MR FRANKLAND, WHO IS STANDING AT HIS GARDEN GATE.
GOOD DAY DR WATSON! I WANTED TO HAVE A WORD WITH YOU.
I HAVE DISCOVERED WHERE THAT CONVICT IS. A BOY IS DELIVERING FOOD TO HIM - UP THERE, ON THE TOR. I HAVE SEEN IT ALL THROUGH MY TELESCOPE.

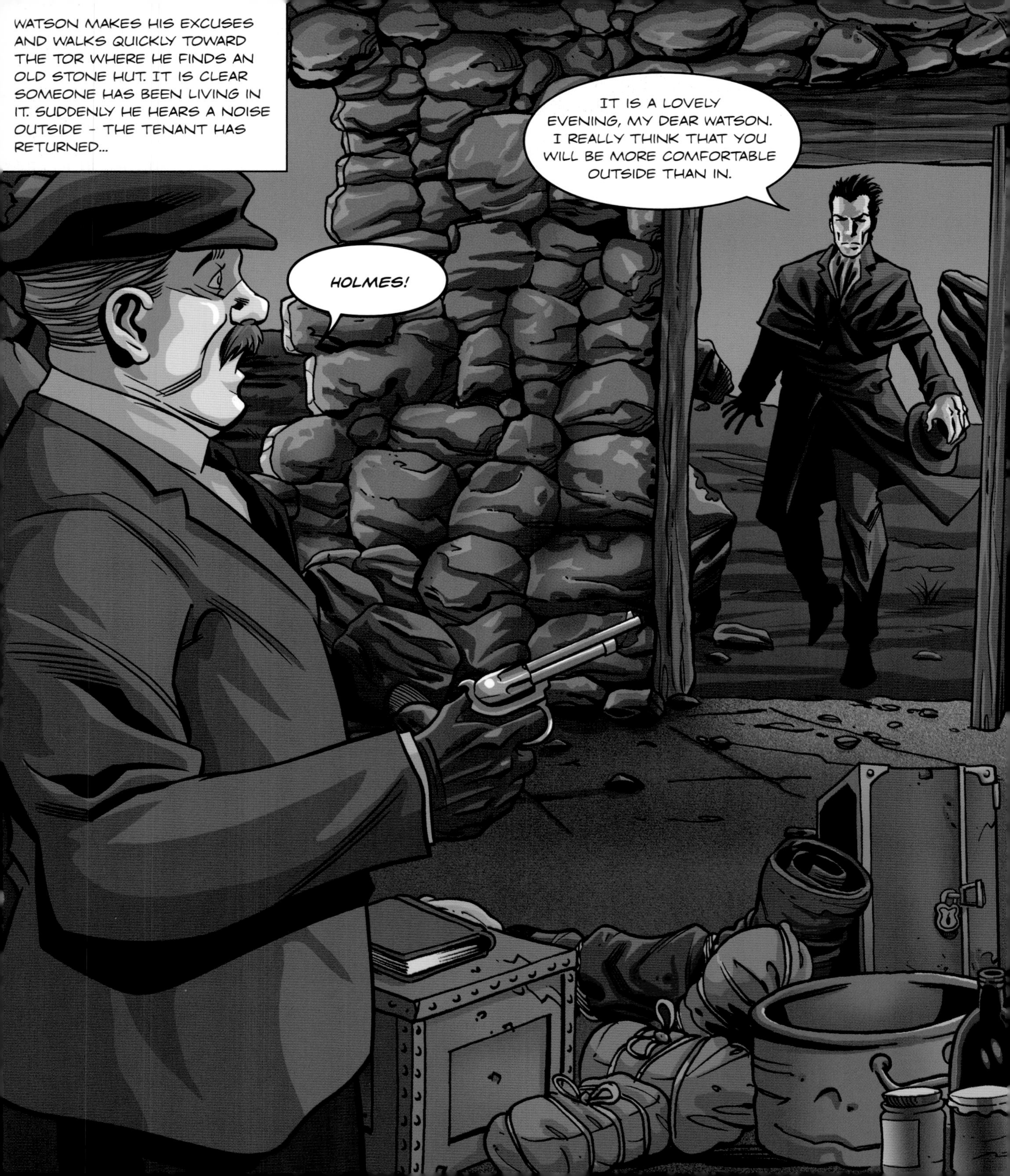
WATSON MAKES HIS EXCUSES AND WALKS QUICKLY TOWARD THE TOR WHERE HE FINDS AN OLD STONE HUT. IT IS CLEAR SOMEONE HAS BEEN LIVING IN IT. SUDDENLY HE HEARS A NOISE OUTSIDE - THE TENANT HAS RETURNED...
IT IS A LOVELY EVENING, MY DEAR WATSON. I REALLY THINK THAT YOU WILL BE MORE COMFORTABLE OUTSIDE THAN IN.
HOLMES!

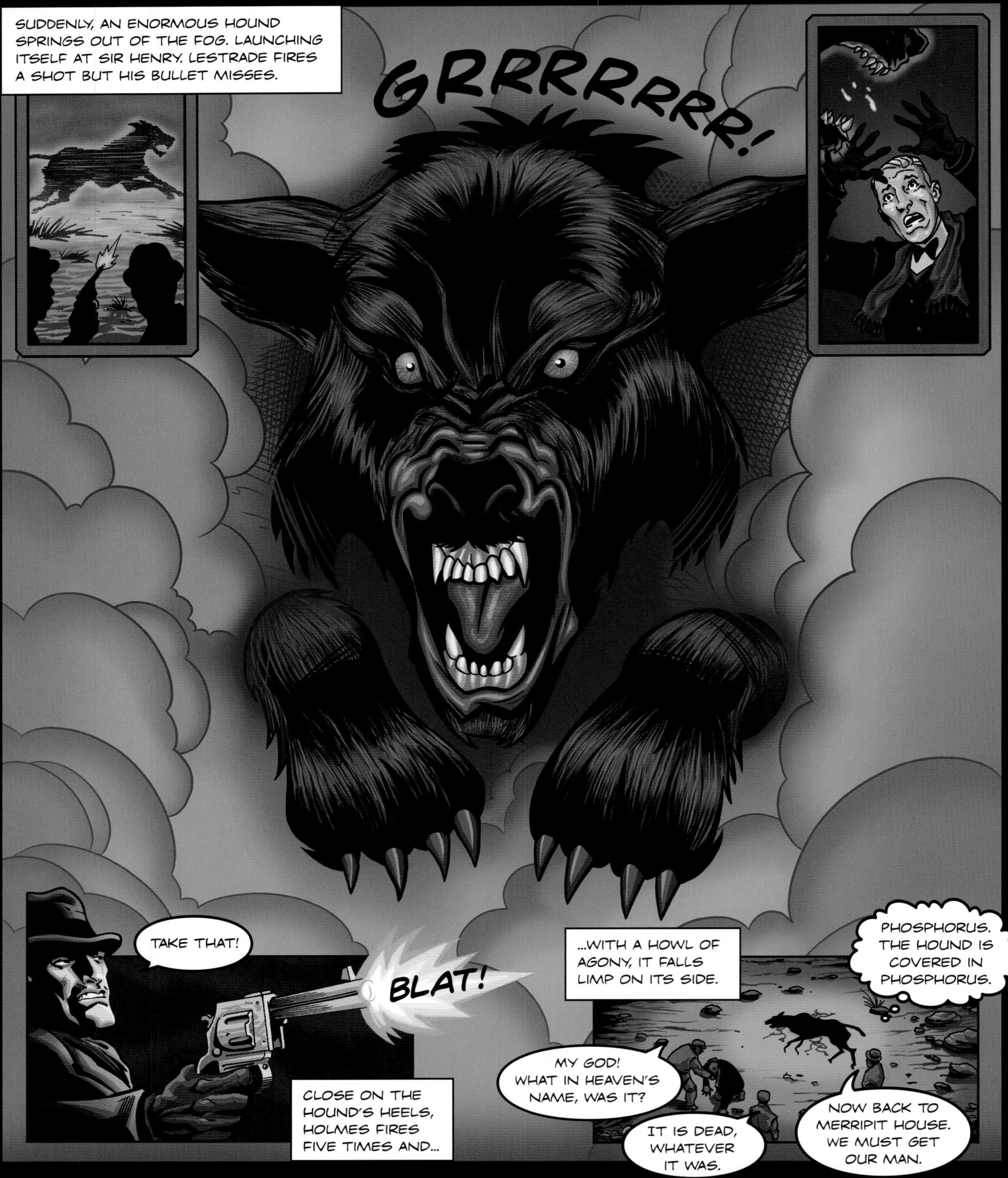
SUDDENLY, AN ENORMOUS HOUND SPRINGS OUT OF THE FOG. LAUNCHING ITSELF AT SIR HENRY. LESTRADE FIRES A SHOT BUT HIS BULLET MISSES.
GRRRRRRR!
TAKE THAT!
BLAT!
CLOSE ON THE HOUND'S HEELS, HOLMES FIRES FIVE TIMES AND...
...WITH A HOWL OF AGONY, IT FALLS LIMP ON ITS SIDE.
PHOSPHORUS. THE HOUND IS COVERED IN PHOSPHORUS.
MY GOD! WHAT IN HEAVEN'S NAME, WAS IT?
IT IS DEAD, WHATEVER IT WAS.
NOW BACK TO MERRIPIT HOUSE. WE MUST GET OUR MAN.

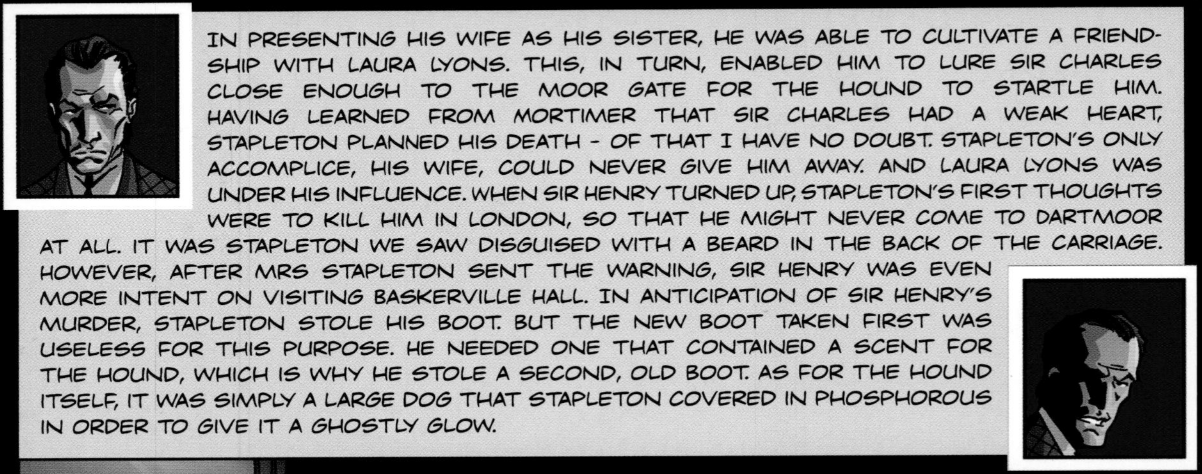
IN PRESENTING HIS WIFE AS HIS SISTER, HE WAS ABLE TO CULTIVATE A FRIENDSHIP WITH LAURA LYONS. THIS, IN TURN, ENABLED HIM TO LURE SIR CHARLES CLOSE ENOUGH TO THE MOOR GATE FOR THE HOUND TO STARTLE HIM. HAVING LEARNED FROM MORTIMER THAT SIR CHARLES HAD A WEAK HEART, STAPLETON PLANNED HIS DEATH - OF THAT I HAVE NO DOUBT. STAPLETON'S ONLY ACCOMPLICE, HIS WIFE, COULD NEVER GIVE HIM AWAY. AND LAURA LYONS WAS UNDER HIS INFLUENCE. WHEN SIR HENRY TURNED UP, STAPLETON'S FIRST THOUGHTS WERE TO KILL HIM IN LONDON, SO THAT HE MIGHT NEVER COME TO DARTMOOR AT ALL. IT WAS STAPLETON WE SAW DISGUISED WITH A BEARD IN THE BACK OF THE CARRIAGE. HOWEVER, AFTER MRS STAPLETON SENT THE WARNING, SIR HENRY WAS EVEN MORE INTENT ON VISITING BASKERVILLE HALL. IN ANTICIPATION OF SIR HENRY'S MURDER, STAPLETON STOLE HIS BOOT. BUT THE NEW BOOT TAKEN FIRST WAS USELESS FOR THIS PURPOSE. HE NEEDED ONE THAT CONTAINED A SCENT FOR THE HOUND, WHICH IS WHY HE STOLE A SECOND, OLD BOOT. AS FOR THE HOUND ITSELF, IT WAS SIMPLY A LARGE DOG THAT STAPLETON COVERED IN PHOSPHOROUS IN ORDER TO GIVE IT A GHOSTLY GLOW.

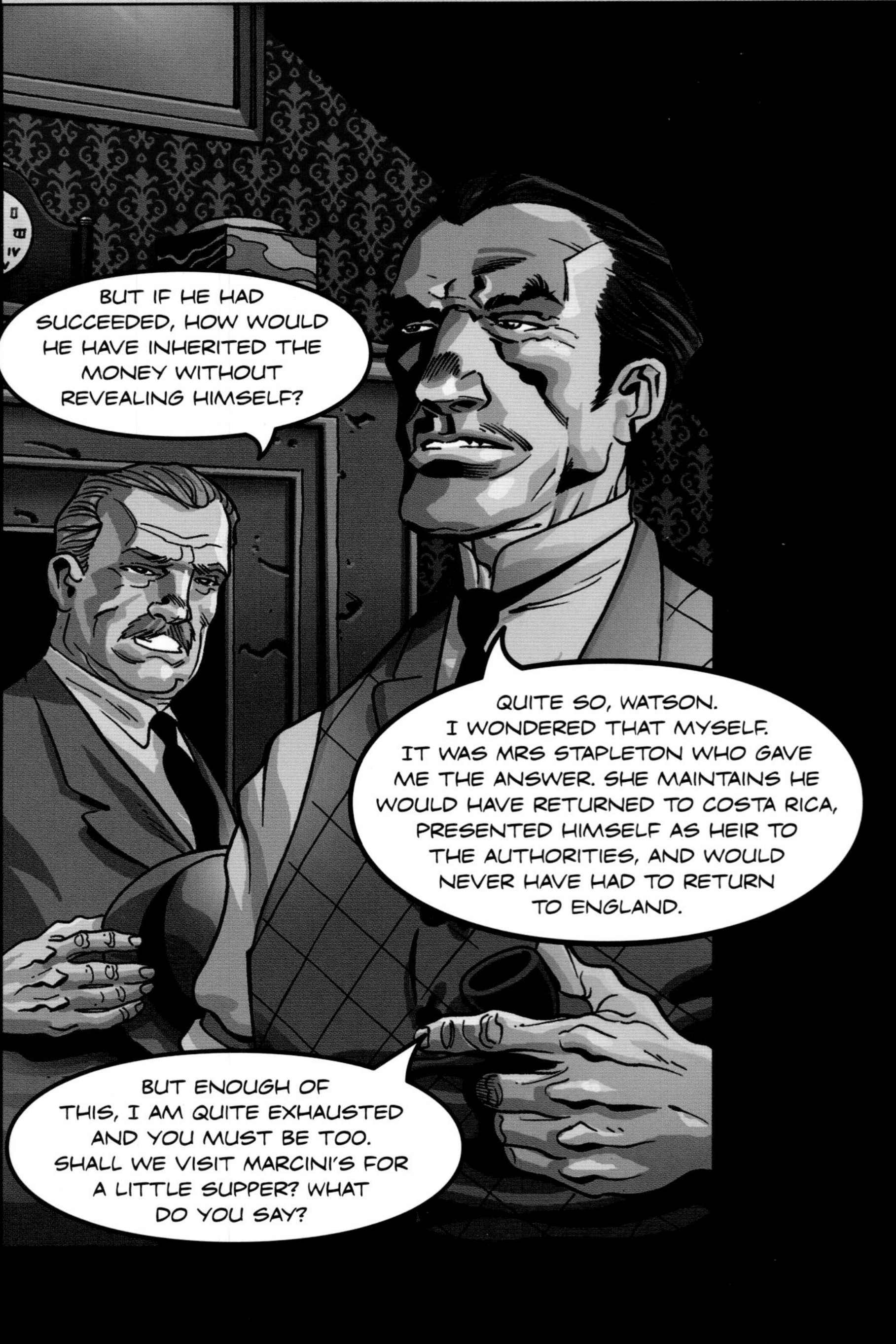
BUT IF HE HAD SUCCEEDED, HOW WOULD HE HAVE INHERITED THE MONEY WITHOUT REVEALING HIMSELF?
QUITE SO, WATSON. I WONDERED THAT MYSELF. IT WAS MRS STAPLETON WHO GAVE ME THE ANSWER. SHE MAINTAINS HE WOULD HAVE RETURNED TO COSTA RICA, PRESENTED HIMSELF AS HEIR TO THE AUTHORITIES, AND WOULD NEVER HAVE HAD TO RETURN TO ENGLAND.
BUT ENOUGH OF THIS, I AM QUITE EXHAUSTED AND YOU MUST BE TOO. SHALL WE VISIT MARCINI'S FOR A LITTLE SUPPER? WHAT DO YOU SAY?

ARCTURUS

THIS EDITION PUBLISHED IN 2014 BY
ARCTURUS PUBLISHING LIMITED
26/27 BICKELS YARD,
151-153 BERMONDSEY STREET,
LONDON SE1 3HA

ISBN: 978-1-78404-357-5
CH004195NT
SUPPLIER 03, DATE 0514, PRINT RUN 3280

STORY: CLAIRE BAMPTON
ART: ANTHONY WILLIAMS
DESIGN: JMS BOOKS
EDITORIAL: KATE OVERY & JOE FULLMAN

PRINTED IN CHINA